SALVAGED HEARTS

HEARTS OF HIDDEN HILLS

SUSAN LOWER

TIME GLIDER BOOKS LLC

Cover designed by Fantasia Frog Designs

This book is a work of fiction. Names, characters, places, and incidents either are products of the author's imagination or are used fictitiously. Any resemblance to actual persons, living or dead, events, or locales is entirely coincidental.

Susan Lower
Visit my website at www.susanlower.com

Printed in the United States of America

First Printing: Apr 2019
Time Glider Books

ISBN-13 978-1-9452748-0-0

SALVAGED HEARTS

Susan Lower

For where your treasure is, there will your heart be also.

—Luke 12:34

1

Bridget Wilson's feet ached. If it weren't for the three blocks left and the temptation of a hot bath beckoning her forward, she would have plopped down on the sidewalk. The satchel hanging from her shoulder bounced against her hip, and the fold-up table in her hand weighed heavier by the minute. Her case slipped from her shoulder as she tripped over the step of the curb in crossing the street. Readjusting her shoulder strap, she spotted a light two-tone blue truck creeping down the back alley of Lexington's less reputable street corners.

She watched as the pickup truck came to a halt in front of a pile of trash. A tall, lean man walked out around the front of the truck. She'd seen his type before, a scavenger rooting through people's trash, looking for scrap metal to trade for cash.

But she couldn't see his face, a shadow in the late July afternoon under the brim of his faded red cap. His jeans had tears at both knees, leaving frayed white threads dangling, and his shirt had a torn pocket. A flap of fabric fell forward as he leaned to inspect an old wingback chair. He tipped it on its side, examining the wooden legs. Then after wrapping his arms around the back of the antique chair, he tossed it into the bed of his truck. She hadn't realized she'd been staring until he glanced at her. Her cheeks flamed. He tipped his hat and grinned.

Bridget fussed over it smoothing down her skirt and pulling at the strap of her bag so it crossed her heart. Her aching calves reminded her of where she was going — home for a hot bath and to soak her feet.

She hoped she'd have enough money to pay her half of the rent this week. Shelby had given her until Friday, but the thirty-eight dollars she'd made in sales wouldn't buy her a night in a motel. She'd spent the morning and most of her afternoon on the corner of Market and Main Street with a case full of kitchen gadgets. Then along came a police officer. She'd given him her usual friendly wave and would have moved on to another spot if not for the heat and her aching feet.

Slowly, the truck pulled away and drove down the alley. Bridget resumed her walk.

What motivated people to dig in smelly old garbage anyway? She shrugged to ease the tension in her shoulders as she stepped onto the sidewalk of her street.

She'd first kick off these horrible heels as soon as she entered the front door.

She passed the tall oaks at the corner of her street. A crowd of people gathered outside her apartment building. Many of them, street scavengers dressed in ragged coats and stolen grocery carts, plowed into one another like hungry kittens trying to get at mother's milk. A stranger held up a red dress, which looked familiar.

Bridget walked faster as a horrible sensation started in the pit of her stomach. She had until Friday, hadn't she?

Her heart pounded. She dropped the folding table and jogged down the street.

Bridget's heart skipped a beat at the sight of the wooden box in an older woman's arms and the black trench coat she bought last year at a yard sale. A man stood trying it on in front of her neighbor's porch. Those were her things!

"Get away!" Bridget ran, waving her arms. She snatched a blouse from the grimy hands of a toothless woman. Several people sauntered away, laughing and tossing snide remarks toward her. She paid no attention. She grabbed the wooden box and tugged, but the old woman held on with the strength of an overprotective mother. "I was here first. Find your own."

"It is my own." Bridget pulled the wooden box toward her.

"Who says?" The old woman yanked the box back in her direction. Her dark hair glinted from days of being unwashed. The rags, which were her clothes, hung to the woman's frame in filth. Had it been anything else in the world, she would have let go.

Bridget spied a man walking up toward a pile of her clothes. "Get away from there."

The man held up his hands, backing away, shaking his head while sidestepping the old woman.

"Let go!" She glared at the woman, her grip on the box tightening. Not this, anything but this …

"Don't put in on the street if you want it," the woman spewed — her breath a furnace of poisonous fumes.

"I live here." Bridget lifted her chin in the direction of the apartment building.

"Not anymore," wheezed an elderly neighbor watching over the dispute from a house next door. Bridget's frosted stare froze his mouth shut.

"Please, it's very special to me." Bridget hoped the old woman would see its sentimental value in the expression of her face.

"Let her have it," another man grumbled, pushing his shopping cart down the street. The woman eyed the box for a second. Then with a huff, she released it. The box tumbled through Bridget's fingers. Sounds of splitting wood echoed in the dead silence of the neighborhood.

Kneeling to pick up the scattered items, she stuffed them into her wooden box as she glimpsed the blue truck. Clutching the splintered wooden lid, she whispered, "I'm sorry, Momma."

From behind her, she heard the old woman make a noise in her throat. Bridget looked up, watching the old woman snatching a suit jacket from a pile of clothes and strutting down the street. Better her coat than her mother's sewing box, she figured, tucking the box under her arm. She walked up onto the porch and pounded on the door. "Shelby!"

Digging into the collar of her blouse, she retrieved her key. Sliding the key into the knob, she tried to turn it. "Couldn't wait to change the locks."

Slapping her hand on the door, she tried to hold herself together.

"Shelby!" She backed down off the porch and onto the sidewalk. "I know you're in there."

The curtains wavered in the second-story window.

"It's not Friday." She stomped her foot. Hot spikes of tears stung her eyes. Her chin trembled, but no matter what, Bridget refused to cry. She wouldn't give the gawking neighbors that satisfaction.

The blue truck pulled alongside the curb, and the stranger got out. He walked around the front of it and leaned against the truck fender with his arms crossed.

"Shelby." Her voice went hoarse with panic. "You can't do this!"

From across the street, an old man came to the porch railing. "Lady, if you don't shut your trap, I'll call the police."

"Mind your own business," Bridget shot back at him. About to say more, she saw the stranger in full view. He tilted down the brim of his ball cap to shade his eyes.

"Got rent?" A painted face with scalloped black hair stuck out through the second-story window.

Bridget stepped away as far as she could without standing on the street, focusing on Shelby. "You said Friday."

"That's what I thought." Shelby retreated.

"You can't do this … I thought we were friends."

Shelby leaned back out. "Friendship doesn't pay the bills."

The cops would come soon enough with the report of a dispute. She wanted no more trouble. She just needed another day … She just needed …

"Throwing me out on the street — is that what friends do?" Hot slices of betrayal cut through her, and the first splashes of tears rolled down her cheeks.

"It's called three months past due." Shelby turned, glancing inside the house. A male voice floated down from the window.

A tidal wave of anger swelled inside her. "Who is that? You got somebody with you?"

"You can't pay!" A hand caught Shelby by the shoulder, pulling her back inside. The disgusting face of Shelby's current fling stuck out in her place.

"Hit the highway." He slammed the window shut before Bridget could respond. She bit her lip. Swiping at the tears trailing down her face, she glared at the swinging curtains. "Well, that's that."

She spun around when the stranger stepped away from his truck. "Hey, what do you think you're doing?"

She propelled herself over what they left of her belongings. The man from the truck paused from loading a bundle of her clothing onto the bed of his truck.

"You don't want any more of your things gone missing, do you?"

"No." She pulled away, keeping her eyes pinned on him.

"Then give me a hand, and I'll give you a lift."

She stared at him a long moment, tried to size him up, and

search his face. What other option did she have? Wearily, she scooped up the remains of her closet, tossed them in the back of the truck, and winced at the smashed stereo. All her CD's stolen or busted.

He lifted the corner of the old wood dresser. Placing her precious wooden box on top, she lifted the other side to aid him in loading it on the truck.

He shut the tailgate and came around to open the passenger side door, tossing the wooden box in on the seat.

She looked at him, saw the same faded cut jeans, the crew neck cotton shirt with the front pocket ripped, and for the first time since she noticed him, she gazed up into his eyes.

Kindness and compassion reflected in their depth.

She expected him to make her feel uncomfortable. But this stranger brought an unusual calm to her wildly beating heart. Perhaps this once, God had sent someone to rescue her. Her knight in shining armor caused her breath to catch when she looked at him. No one had ever looked at her that way.

She reached into her blouse, pulling the cord from her neck. The small silver key gleamed in her hand. Looking up at the window, she raised the loop off her head and tossed the key at the porch.

He stood, holding the truck's passenger door open for her.

She climbed into the truck's cab, hoisted her satchel on the seat, and pulled the wooden box onto her lap.

The door creaked shut. She pulled the visor low, keeping her face blocked from the neighbors who stood across the street, gawking at her.

He slid in the seat beside her, and a moment later, she heard the truck's engine come to life. She watched from the passenger window as the last place she called home faded from her view.

Sounds of police sirens blared in the distance.

What would she do now? There had to be a better way for a

girl to make a living than selling magnets and dollar store spatulas. She'd sold all those frilly fans she'd made and had thirty-eight dollars for her trouble. She shouldn't have expected any different.

Nevertheless, on the third day of the month, she knew people brought stuff with their social security checks and welfare payments. People should have been out cashing their checks and running errands. But not today, not when she needed to pitch her sale on them.

She clutched the wooden box and stared ahead.

"Got any place I can drop you off?"

She didn't know. "A shelter, maybe?"

She had never wanted to go back there. But what choice did she have? When Granny died, she'd tried to keep things afloat. They hadn't owned the house they'd lived in, and the landlord had been kind enough to give Bridget a few extra months to put her affairs in order. With a high school diploma and an old sewing machine, she planned to make it on her own. Except, years later, she found she wasn't any better off than those who stood in line at the soup kitchens where she regularly volunteered.

Thirty-eight dollars wasn't enough to buy her a bed for one night and would leave her with an empty stomach the next morning.

"Friends? Family?" he asked.

"I think you just saw what friends do," she whispered. How could Shelby toss her out like that? It had to be the new boyfriend, Dan. Or was it Duke? Not that it mattered. Shelby had always been willing to accept small payments on the rent until now.

"Family?"

She had a mother, somewhere, that she hadn't seen or heard from since she'd been eight. And as far as a father went, her mother had never given her a name. She doubted her mother even knew, which left her mother's brother, who, last time she checked, had another eight years of prison left. The only one she could ever count on had been Granny.

"Nope." She leaned against the door, looking out the passenger side window.

"I see." He headed south onto the highway.

"No, you don't, but that's okay. Nobody's asking you to."

"I'm sure there's someone," he said.

In less than a year, she'd lost everything — family, home, and job.

"There isn't," she snapped, irate at his persistence. "I'm not a kid; I can take care of myself."

Momentarily, his eyes left the road to glance at her. When he looked back, he said, "No, you're not."

Her cheeks warmed. She shouldn't have snapped at Luke like that. It wasn't his fault she couldn't pay half the rent. Nor was it his fault that she'd fallen into a pit of financial despair this past year.

Her mother always said she was too trusting. "Where are you taking me?"

"Hidden Hills."

"Is there a shelter there?" she asked.

"No, but I know a place where you can stay."

She didn't respond. Her gaze shifted back out the window. Endless buildings lit up their commercial signs preparing for the impending darkness of evening.

"I'm Bridget," she said finally, watching the distance expand between her and the city.

"Luke Myers."

2

Luke kept one eye on the road and one on his passenger. She sat with her arms wrapped around the broken wooden box as if it were life's breath, staring ahead.

He hadn't been looking for a woman. He wasn't sure what he'd been looking for after he'd left Children's Hospital.

But he found her. Dark strands of hair framed her face, and a small hair clip dangled at the nape of her neck.

"Hard to believe a woman like you would find herself out on the street."

She turned her head and glared at him. "I would have had the money come Friday."

"Three months' worth?" He hated getting involved with other people's problems, but this one was unavoidable. From the moment he laid eyes on her walking down the street, he'd felt drawn to her.

"It's Wednesday. Nobody buys stuff on the street on Wednesdays."

"You're a street vendor?"

"Yeah, so?" She tilted her chin up. He'd hit a nerve. Her eyes narrowed. "At least you don't see me digging in people's garbage."

He bit back the reply that first came to mind and said instead, "You know what they say … one man's trash is another man's treasure."

His father used to say it all the time. He had been a salvage collector dealing in used farm equipment and old cars for nearly thirty years before a massive heart attack took his father home to Jesus.

Luke was glad none of his old teammates could see him now. They had given him a hard time when he left playing in the major leagues to go home and care for his family. He hadn't the heart to return after putting his mother in a local nursing home last year.

He wasn't cut out to make a profit like his father. How quick he had been to give in to every sob story and heartbreak situation. He barely sold a car for profit. Now, instead of cars and old tractors, Luke found his treasures elsewhere like the chair in the back of his truck.

"It's respectable," she said with a hint of defense.

"Sure." He flicked on his turn signal. Darkness would soon settle over the horizon. Ordinarily, he would have turned on the radio, but he figured the silence would allow him to think.

She turned her face away, but not before he saw a tear rolling down her cheek.

He'd dealt with enough weeping females to know that sometimes it was best to let them cry.

These kinds of tears conned men into doing things for women. Hadn't that been why he'd driven the entire way out here?

It was for the town, a desperate mother, and a little boy that he'd driven to Lexington. Tears or no tears, Luke would have come to Children's Hospital to see the boy.

Jimmy was one of his Little League players. Luke had delivered gifts, cards, and an envelope filled with cash to the boy and the boy's mother from the little town of Hidden Hills.

Luke wasn't fooled. She could deny it all she wanted, but

he knew Sonya, Jimmy's mother, hadn't left the boy's room for days. As he knew, the woman sitting beside him would have slept on the street tonight.

He clicked on his low beams watching the road out ahead. Bridget huddled against the passenger side door, wiping her tears with the sleeve of her shirt. He wished he could offer her a tissue or even a kind word. But he wasn't sure anything he said would erase the dejected expression he saw on her face through the shadows of the truck cab.

"You might as well settle in. It's a long ride to Hidden Hills."

She reached up, pulled the dangling hair clip from her hair, and leaned against the seat. Her gaze was directed out the window.

He figured her attitude would change as he drove away from the city. His stomach grumbled, reminding him he hadn't eaten since taking Jimmy's mother to the hospital cafeteria for lunch. Not knowing when the last time Bridget had eaten either, he pulled off the highway and drove through the nearest fast-food joint.

"Keep it." She'd reached into her bag and pulled out her wallet. Luke slid two wrapped burgers in her direction. She eyed them, looked up at him again, and still held out the money. "You can pay me back later."

Satisfied with his response, Bridget put the money in her wallet and picked up the first of the burgers. She held onto it for a moment, closed her eyes, and peeled down the wrapper after a second or two. "How long before we're there?"

"A couple of hours." He bit into his burger, pulling onto the highway again.

"You came awful far to pick up some junk."

In the flashing lights of the shadows, he watched from the corner of his eye as she picked the tomatoes off her burger. "Sometimes, the most precious things can be found in the most unlikely places."

"An old chair?"

He finished his burger before he spoke. "An old chair, a beautiful lady, a hurt kid who probably won't ever throw a baseball again." His voice trailed off as he looked out into the darkness of the highway.

She said nothing for a long while.

Luke was grateful for the stretch of silence. He couldn't get over seeing Jimmy laying there in that hospital bed, a prune of a boy who just days earlier was bursting with life. He didn't have to see the expression on Sonya's face to know she felt guilty. A mother whose heart swelled with regret, that if she had paid more attention ... just for a minute ... she wouldn't have agreed to whatever Jimmy had said.

Luke sighed.

"Will he be okay?" Bridget asked. "You know, the boy who won't throw a baseball again?"

Luke gripped the steering wheel. "That depends on what you mean by 'okay,' but he'll live."

The bits of his second burger burned in his gut like a pit of lava. Jimmy knew better than to play with fire, but his mother had said it was okay.

"You drove out here to visit the boy in the hospital. That's nice," she said, resting her head on the window. After a bit, she dozed off.

Hours later, Luke pulled into a gravel driveway and parked in front of an old barn across the road from the dark frame of a house. She looked over at him. Panic shone in her eyes.

"You can stay here." He turned the key, killing the ignition. He pushed open the door and came around to her side of the truck. She stared at him, her eyes large and round and frightened.

"If you think ..." she began as he opened her door.

"I don't," he quickly cut her off.

Slowly, she slid from the truck, keeping her gaze fixed on

him. He stood holding the door open. She backed away from him. Her shoes crunched in the gravel. "All the same, I think I'll find my own place."

"Going door to door at this time?" he asked.

"I can take care of myself."

He saw her determined stance and didn't doubt that she could.

"Thanks for the ride." She pushed passed him.

"What about your stuff?" He bit the inside corner of his lip, trying to mask his amusement.

"You can have it. There's nothing there I can't replace."

Liar. She had fought hard to keep hold of her wooden box. She wouldn't leave it any more than the other stuff on the back of his truck.

She turned and walked away.

"Don't forget to knock," he called. He stifled a few chuckles.

Luke gave her a few feet head start as she crossed the road. Her ankle twisted in the gravel drive, and the heel of her shoe snapped. Her knees hit the road pavement first, and then her hands took the brunt of her fall.

Lengthening his strides, he was beside her in an instant. He reached down and grasped her by the elbow. She jerked her arm away and stood up. Tears prickled her eyes. She grabbed her bag, which had fallen into the middle of the road. She limped toward the house.

A pair of headlights shone down the road, and a car approached her.

He grabbed her again, pulling her backward. Her back pressed to his chest for a moment as the car sped past. He breathed in her lavender scented perfume. Bridget pushed away and stepped off the street and into the edge of the lawn. He followed behind her.

When he reached for her again, she evaded him. "Don't touch me."

He held his hands up. Bridget whirled around. "Don't follow me, either!"

Luke stopped, allowing her to stagger a few steps ahead of him again. He watched as she made her way to the concrete slab porch. He took a few more steps forward.

"Listen, pal, I've already told you. I'm not interested." Her voice raised to a high squeak.

Luke shook his head. He stuck his hands in his pockets and stood where he was, watching as she took another step closer to the front door. The porch light switched on, outlining their shadows against the bushes by the walk.

She pulled back her shoulders and knocked. "I don't need an audience."

He stepped up onto the porch and leaned against a white column holding the porch roof overhead. "Suit yourself."

She raised her hand to knock again. The door opened. Startled, she stood poised like a statue. A woman with long dark hair raised her eyebrows.

Slowly, Bridget's face molded into a smile. As she opened her mouth to speak, the other woman said, "I wondered if you were back yet. The girls have eaten already. I was just going to put your supper in the microwave when I heard a knock."

Luke stepped in front of Bridget. Her jaw dropped and hung slack. He almost reached out and picked it up for her.

"I had a full load today," Luke said.

"Another stray?"

Bridget turned to hobble away, but he reached out and took hold of her arm. "Sort of."

He leaned in the doorway. "Got enough for two?"

Bridget yanked her arm, but he didn't let go.

The other woman scowled at them.

"Coming?" He looked at Bridget. She stood staring at him as if he were the cat who'd just caught the mouse. "If you'd rather stay outside …"

She shook her head, speechless.

He pressed his hand to the small of her back and led her inside. Sounds of a television drifted in from a nearby room. Bridget eased her satchel to the floor next to her shoes.

"There are leftovers in the fridge. Your plate should be warm," the woman said, leaving them in the room alone.

Luke took the plate and sat it on the table before her. He motioned for her to sit. She was bone thin and probably hadn't had a decent meal in who knows when not counting the burgers they had in the truck. However, right as he might have been, she couldn't resist the inviting smells of pork roast and mashed potatoes, and neither could he.

He pulled out the cold leftovers and reheated them in the microwave. He heard Bridget scrape her fork over the plate. His gaze shifted to where she sat, and he watched as she pulled her long dark curly tresses away from her shoulders. She wasn't at all the way he'd pictured a homeless person. Though technically she'd been homeless for over two hours, he couldn't picture someone as lovely as her without a home. He also couldn't picture someone like her walking the street of Lexington alone.

He hadn't intended to scavenge this day. He had plenty in his garage from previous expeditions. And he'd gone, anyway. Call it a feeling or spiritual intuition. No matter the reason, he'd found something irreplaceable.

He poured them a glass of milk and clanked one down in front of her. From just around the doorway, the woman said, "There's pie on the counter."

"Thanks, Lisa," he said.

He sat down across from Bridget. She mumbled something incoherent and cast her eyes to her plate. She'd scraped it clean like he figured she would and gulped down the milk.

He tilted on his chair and reached for the pie on the counter. She looked up, watching as he sat the pie down between them.

"You read my mind."

"My mom used to say, 'There's always room for dessert.'"

That made her smile. He pushed the pie toward her as he took the first bite of pork off his plate. He watched her take a slice of Dutch apple pie and place it in front of her. When she'd finished eating, he asked, "More?"

"No, thank you."

"Are you sure?" He took away her empty dishes, piling them in the sink.

"Finished?" Lisa returned to the kitchen, standing in the doorway. She crossed her arms and leaned against the jam.

"It was delicious. Thank you," Bridget said.

Bridget looked between him and Lisa. "Um ... do you mind if I use your bathroom?"

"Down the hall." Luke pointed past Lisa. Bridget rose, and Lisa stepped far enough away to give her space to pass.

"Second door to your left." Waiting until she heard the door click shut, Lisa walked into the kitchen. "Since when do you pick up people?"

Luke turned on the faucet, rinsing the dishes. "She had no place to go." He took their plates and put them in the dishwasher.

"And you brought her here?"

"She would have gone to a shelter."

"Then why didn't you let her?" Lisa asked.

Luke looked over his shoulder. "You ever been to a shelter?"

"Of course not!"

"They're not nice places. Homeless men and women sleeping on floors huddled in borrowed blankets. If you're lucky, you can find a cot or sometimes a breakfast. And, if you're fortunate, they give you a bagged lunch before sending you off till night comes again to wander the streets."

"Isn't that where you found her? On a street corner somewhere?" Lisa walked over and shut the dishwasher door when Luke reached for it.

"Not exactly." He leaned against the sink, unsure why he needed to explain himself to his sister.

"Then how is it exactly?" She switched on the dishwasher.

"When I first spotted her, she was going door to door through the residential district carrying a satchel. She was trying to sell some kind of product."

"Most Avon ladies don't go knocking these days," Lisa said.

"All her belongings, or most of them anyway, were thrown out on the sidewalk in front of an apartment building. People were sorting through and stealing her stuff when I came upon her a second time."

"And you couldn't resist stopping." Lisa leaned against the counter.

"She was fighting a bag lady over a large wooden box."

"Sounds like a real winner," Lisa muttered.

"The fact is she's got nowhere to go or anyone to help her, Lisa. She couldn't pay her rent, so her roommate tossed her out. There is no reason we can't help her."

"Fine. Give her twenty bucks and send her on her way."

Luke's hands clenched into fists. "She can stay here."

"Are you crazy? No! Absolutely not!" Lisa kept her voice low to a harsh whisper. She glanced down the hall. "You don't know this woman. She could be a thief or a con artist. She could be a murderess, for all you know."

"I told you what I know. She can stay in the RV if you don't let her stay here," Luke said.

"That old camper of yours? I've got two kids to think about." Lisa slapped her hand on the counter, making her point clear.

"The RV it is." He pushed away from the counter.

"She'll stay one night and be gone with whatever she can put in her pockets. You'll see."

When Luke didn't respond, Lisa said, "Do you even know her name?"

"Bridget."

"Does she have a last name?" Lisa asked.

"Probably. Most people do." He glanced down the hallway once more.

"You don't know?" Lisa hissed. "Why does this not surprise me?" She strutted across the kitchen, bending over to retrieve Bridget's satchel. Luke came up behind her and snatched it away.

"I'm just going to check her bag for ID."

"I heard something about my bag," Bridget stood in the kitchen's entrance from the hallway.

Ignoring Lisa's sharp glare in his direction, Luke handed Bridget her bag. "Here you go. Wouldn't want anyone to trip over it."

3

Bridget sensed the awkward shift in the air, like a window shutting off a spring breeze from inside the kitchen. She'd heard their voices from inside the bathroom. But, she could no longer tolerate the biting sensation of her scraped knee, any more than the tone of Lisa's voice. It would be best if she left.

Bridget cleansed her knee, washing off the dirt and rubble embedded from the road with a washcloth by the sink. After searching the medicine cabinet, she found a bandage. She didn't enjoy going through other people's things, but; she felt awkward and ashamed having to ask for something so basic as a Band-Aid.

"You've got blood on your leg!" a small voice said just before a little girl bound out of a room across the hall. Bridget managed a smile for the little girl. Her feathered blond hair cascaded around her small round face. Big blue eyes dampened with tears.

"It's alright." Her attempt to cleanse the wounds had only made them bleed more.

"Did you fall?" Another little girl, older, almost identical to the first, stepped around her.

"You need a Band-Aid."

"Angie …. Lizzy …. You two should go back to bed," Lisa said.

"Does it hurt?" the first little girl asked, ignoring her mother's request.

"It's just a scratch." Bridget waved it off. She'd sat throughout supper, hoping she could ignore the pain by stuffing her face. Ignore the man sitting across from her and forget he had a wife. Not to mention two kids.

"We've got Band-Aids." The second little girl ran down the hallway.

"Lizzy …" Lisa gave the little girl a stern look.

"I'm fine. It's just a scrape." But before she could protest further, the first little girl and Luke inspected her knee. Both the expressions on the girl's and Luke's faces twisted her gut. All she wanted to do was get out of there before she felt any more humiliated than she already did.

"Here." The older girl, Angie, held out a box of Band-Aids.

"I'll take care of her. You two run off to bed now," Luke said.

"But it's too early!" A set of small arms crossed, and little lips pouted.

"Come on, girls." Lisa directed them back into their room.

"I'll just be going now." Bridget took her cue to leave. Lisa's dark penetrating glare over her shoulder made her quiver. She stepped into the wall of Luke's chest as he blocked her path. Sharply, she breathed in. His towering presence loomed over her, and she gazed up at him.

"And where would that be?" he asked.

"I'll find a place." She tried to step around him.

"First, let's take care of those scrapes. Then I'll take you to a place."

She shivered at the tone of his voice. By his expression, she knew he wouldn't budge. She stomped over to her shoes, which she had left at the front door, and slid them on. She picked up her satchel, and he handed her the box of Band-Aids.

"The welcome mat's been pulled." She grabbed her satchel from his hand. Hefting it over her shoulder, she paused and stared at him. "Are you listening to me?"

"I heard you." He brushed past her and held open the door. "This way."

"I'm not one for trouble." She stepped outside the house.

He shut the door and walked past her into the darkness. "Could have fooled me."

She followed, crossing the lawn after him. Together they walked across the street to an old barn with an RV parked alongside it. She halted, stepping onto the gravel parking lot. In the field near to the RV sat shells of old cars and machinery with tall grasses growing up over them.

The next nearest house sat down the road several yards. She ignored the stinging in her knee. Tears threatened to spill onto her lashes. This was it. She had no other place to go, at *least for tonight.*

"Over here," Luke walked in the truck's direction. He shrugged when she didn't move from beneath the glow of the light post. Bridget turned and rubbed her arms against the goosebumps prickling her arms. Listening, she heard the tailgate of the truck drop. Sounds of metal rollers groaning on their track racked the night like a pair of fingernails on a chalkboard.

She gritted her teeth. Dipping her head, she should be grateful. Sighing, she turned and watched him unload his truck. He pushed open the big sliding door of the barn and set her belongings inside. He struggled with the small dresser she'd gotten last year from a neighbor who moved and couldn't take it with them. Lights flooded from inside, shying away the darkness.

She walked up to the truck, scooping up the last bunch of clothes. A girl needed an extra outfit, didn't she?

"I figured you'd change your mind." He closed the tailgate.

Her shoulders slumped. She could have done without it. Sshe could.

"Follow me." He led her around the side of the barn. She shivered more uncontrollably than the last time as they left the light of the lamppost. He opened the door to an old model RV and flipped on the light inside.

Every nerve in her body screamed for her to run. The fact he was married brought little comfort.

"Home sweet home." He grinned.

Slowly, she stepped up into the RV. As he entered behind her, the trailer shifted with his weight on the stair.

She tossed her clothes in a pile on the floor just inside the doorway.

"Couch pulls out to a bed. The fridge is on the blink, but the stove works. There's a bathroom around the corner. I'll get the water hooked up in the morning."

"Thank you." She held her breath, waiting for him to leave.

"Just make yourself at home." He moved through the space, hunching down by the far wall and pulling out a drawer from a built-in cabinet. When he turned around, he held a first-aid kit in his hand.

She backed up and found her legs buckling as she plopped into the sofa. "W-what are you d-doing?"

He bent down in front of her.

"These cuts are pretty deep," he said.

"But I have Band-Aids." Or she had. She must have dropped them with her clothes at the front door.

His hand swept up her calf, spreading warmth past her knee.

"You don't have to do that." She sat at the edge of her seat. He was a married man. Silently, she repeated that — over and over.

"Just take it easy." He flipped open the kit. He dabbed peroxide on her wound. She hissed as the liquid fizzled over her cuts. Gently, he brushed away her hands as she reached for it. A flush of warmth crept up her neck and spread across her cheeks as he blew softly on her knee. She waited for him to finish as he placed a large bandage across it.

His hands skimmed down her leg and over her ankle, flopping off her shoe. Alarmed, she drew back her leg.

"Relax. You've been on your feet all day." He pressed his thumbs into the arch of her foot. She nearly groaned from the sheer pleasure of his fingers, relieving the ache she'd felt all evening. But this was wrong. Why else would it feel so good? His fingers found all the right pressure points. And here she was with thirty-eight dollars to her name, homeless, and another woman's husband rubbing her feet.

She jolted, pulling her foot away.

"You okay?" His head rose, looking up at her closely from beneath the brim of his cap.

"I ... you don't have to do this."

His answer was to take off the shoe on her other foot and press his thumbs into her arch. "I don't mind."

She bit her lip. He had a family with two beautiful little girls and a wife. "Those were sweet little girls."

"Lizzy and Angie." He continued to massage her foot.

"You must be very proud."

"Yep, Lisa's got her hands full with those two. Lizzy is three, and Angie is six next month."

"Sounds like they keep you on your toes." Maybe if she kept talking, the enjoyment of his hands would go away.

"Their parents, yes. I just spoil them and send them home."

"Parents? But aren't you ..." She pulled her foot away and stared at him.

He chuckled. "Their uncle. Lisa is my sister."

"Oh." That was all she could say. She watched him stand and put the first-aid kit away.

"There are blankets in the cabinet here if you get cold. I suppose I could get you a fan in here if it gets too hot, being July. I'll see you in the morning."

"You're not afraid I might steal you blind in the middle of the night and run off?"

He winced. "I'm sorry you heard that."

"Wilson. My name is Bridget Wilson."

"You don't have to tell me any of those things."

She did. He'd humbled her, kneeling and ministering to her feet and wounds. She'd expected him to toss the first-aid kit at her and leave or demand some kind of payment for the things he'd done for her today. But he hadn't.

She couldn't blame his sister for not trusting a stranger in their house.

"Don't worry. When I leave, I'll only take what's mine."

The following day, Bridget rose before the sun. She hadn't been able to sleep. Not without the sounds of the city. The silence of being out in the middle of nowhere disturbed her. She'd strained her neck, listening, waiting. Just once she heard a car down the road. During the night, she listened to what could have been an animal rattling something metal. She tensed and waited for it to go away, but not before checking the RV door to ensure it was locked.

Taking a deep breath of the clean air, she sat on the doorstep of the RV. From behind the trees, the sun's rising glow cast over the junk in the field. Down along the road and around the barn, she saw a fence.

Clearly, she'd been distressed and not thinking right when she got in a truck with a stranger and came here. She could have ended up in a far worse situation, and Bridget's cheeks warmed a little more with the memory of Luke's hands on her feet. Oh yes, much worse, she patted her aching knee.

She sorted through her clothes and took only the best garments she could stuff into a small bag. She folded up the bed and returned the cushions to the couch. Satisfied that everything was returned to its place, she glanced at the wooden box, her fingers itching to pick it up. Deep inside, she knew it would be better to leave it. With a great sigh, she adjusted the satchel on her shoulder. It wasn't like she had anywhere to go. It would be there when she got back.

Where ever she was going, she didn't yet know. She walked the opposite way from the house she'd visited the previous night.

She walked around the barn and a small cement block building with a sign on the door that said closed. Dirt and rock covered a small lane and parking behind the block building. A dozen goats and three horses grazed between the abandoned machines parked out in the grassy fields.

Several yards away from the block extension of the barn, a red metal garage sat with Luke's blue truck parked in front of the large sliding door.

Inside the garage, she found him dissecting an appliance. He had a smear of grease by his nose and looked up at her. "Have a nice sleep?"

"There's nothing around here for miles, is there?" she asked.

"People."

"Town? You know, a place with buses and taxis … transportation."

"No buses, no taxis …"

She stared at him, her brain digesting his words. No taxis, no buses?

"No homeless shelters, either," he told her.

She felt the color drain from her face. "Why did you bring me here?"

He regarded her a moment. "Where else would you have gone?"

She'd been kicked to the curb like an old piece of trash, and he'd salvaged her.

"Besides, something told me you needed a friend."

"I think I'm done having friends." A bitter taste came to her mouth as she thought of Shelby. They'd been friends since high school, and look where that friendship got her.

"Maybe you haven't had the right kind of friends." Luke looked at his half-torn-apart washing machine and picked up a screwdriver. "You ought to give people a chance."

She'd given him a chance, and right now, Luke was the closest thing she had to a friend. A little scared by it, she turned and inspected the place. "So, is this your place?"

Luke paused from twisting another screw loose inside the machine. "You could say that."

She got the feeling Luke said little at all.

Bridget stepped closer to him. "Mind if I ask what you do here?"

"I keep the place running." Luke went back to wiggling some wires and slipped his hand deeper into the machine's metal guts.

"Okay." Bridget clasped her hands together. "I take it you like to fix things? This is a repair shop?"

Luke cursed under his breath, and Bridget went rigid.

"It belonged to my dad. Lots of folks looking for used parts to fix farm equipment and whatnot."

"I see business is booming in these parts."

He snorted. She hadn't meant it as an insult. Bridget stepped away, afraid she should shut her trap and move on before she caused more trouble.

"There are clean towels in the RV. I hooked up the water earlier and turned on the propane if you want to shower. There is some hot coffee brewing over by the office, along with donuts." He tossed the screwdriver to the side and withdrew a long metal rod from the washing machine. "I take it you didn't have breakfast. We can go later to grab some groceries to stock in there for you."

"Office?"

"The old milk house."

He must have read the bewildered look on her face, for he pointed and said, "Block building by the barn. The door's unlocked."

"Thank you." She walked to the old milk house. Inside sat a table with a coffee machine percolating and a box of glazed donuts. She glanced over her shoulder.

Alone, she picked up a donut and then another. Pouring herself a hot cup of coffee in a mug, she set out from the block building to her little RV beside the barn. It wouldn't hurt to shower first and figure out what to do next second.

4

"Whatcha doin'?" Lizzy asked, skipping into the old machine shed.

Luke leaned against the washing machine. "You look pretty this morning."

Lizzy grinned, too young for blushing and never a shy one. She hugged his leg. He reached over and wiped off his hands before scooping her up into a bear hug against his chest.

Behind her, Lisa stepped into the shed with Angie lingering at the door. "It's not noon, and you're tearing something apart again."

Luke shifted Lizzy in his arms. Her chubby little hands held onto his neck, and she laid her head on his shoulder. "I've almost got it fixed."

Lisa rolled her eyes. "Does it at least wash clothes?"

"Of course it does." He'd made a few adjustments, that's all.

Improvements, he liked to say, which had become his signature around town. Putting things back together the way they were didn't provide much of a challenge. Creating something new from something old now that put fire in his blood.

"And what else does it do?" Lisa walked over and laid her hand on the old washing machine.

He held Lizzy with one arm and lifted a lid on the side of the machine. He'd spent the morning attaching it.

"Great, what every washing machine needs, another lid. Anyway, I need you to watch Lizzy while I take Angie to an appointment and run some errands," Lisa said.

He heard the door shut with a quiet click on the other side of the machine shed. "Sure."

His gaze fell on Bridget, dressed in an old pair of torn jeans and a sleeveless shirt. She'd left her damp hair hanging loose down over her shoulders.

"Didn't I see her leave this morning?" Lisa asked, keeping her tone low.

Bridget stood, hovering at the door that she'd just come through.

Lizzy slipped down from his arms and ran toward Bridget.

"What can I say? I'm irresistible." Luke shrugged.

Lisa shook her head. "I suppose I could take her with me, drop her off with Pastor Lawrence, and let him deal with her."

Luke's hand shot out and gripped his sister's arm as she turned toward Bridget. "Now, why would you do that?"

Lisa glanced down at where his hand gripped her arm and back up at his face. "You can't play the knight in shining armor forever. Picking up other people's junk and fixing it is one thing, but picking up women off the street is best left to the church."

"You and I both know that Pastor Lawrence will take her downtown, give her a meal, and take her to the nearest town with a homeless shelter. Back, right where I found her, and have gained nothing."

He glanced over at Bridget, who frowned, watching them. Yet, as Lizzy approached, Bridget smiled wearily and bent down to listen to the little girl talk.

"So? What is it to you?" Lisa asked.

How could he explain that yesterday he'd been on autopilot? He'd always kept to the city's northern district, but something had drawn him south. He glanced at Bridget, tucking a strand of hair behind her ear.

He released Lisa and cleared his throat. "She can stay here."

"Perhaps you should talk to Pastor Lawrence about this homeless shelter you've started," Lisa said, turning away. "Lizzy, I'm leaving."

"Bye, Mom!" Lizzy waved.

Lisa frowned and looked at Luke again before taking Angie by the hand and walking out of the garage.

Bridget straightened, and Lizzy took her by the hand, leading her closer to Luke. "See what Luke is fixing."

"It's a washing machine," Bridget said. "Listen, if you'll just take me to the nearest town with a bus stop, I'll be out of your hair."

Luke bent down and tugged on the edge of Lizzy's dress. He tilted his head toward the door Bridget had just come out of. "There are donuts on the table."

Lizzy's eyes grew enormous, and she raced off in the direction he indicated.

She had no place to go, no family. Hadn't she said so? "Don't pay Lisa any mind. She wasn't always like this. Tough times do funny things to people. Closes their hearts and makes them hard."

"Really? I wouldn't know," she said, almost sarcastically.

"Give Lisa some time. She'll come around." Luke heard the door open and watched as Lizzy came walking out into the garage with a glazed donut in hand.

"I don't plan on being here that long," Bridget said.

"And where will you go?" He walked to the other side of the washer, pretending to inspect his work while waiting for his pulse to steady.

"Louisville, maybe? A friend of mine moved out there a couple of years ago."

"Ever hear from that friend?"

She bit her lip and shook her head.

"What's wrong with right here?" he asked. The sight of her tossed across her belongings on the street flashed in his mind. He wanted her to stay.

Lizzy stood beside her and slipped her tiny hand into Bridget's. He smiled as Lizzy stared up at Bridget with sugar glaze on her face.

Bridget sighed. "What am I supposed to do in a place like this? I can't sleep in your RV forever."

"You're right." And the more he wanted her to stay, he knew it would be best if she left. For all she saw of him was a man who picked up junk. But, he could hope.

Stepping around the washing machine and pulling a rag from his back pocket to clean his hands, he said, "But at least here, you've got a start."

By mid-morning, Lizzy got restless, and Bridget had never been in a place where she didn't know what to do.

Lizzy huffed down on the ground, crossing her little legs and resting her chin in her hands. "I'm bored."

"You can help me unload the truck," Luke offered. He'd finished with the washing machine, and between answering the cordless phone in his back pocket and searching for parts on the storage shelves lining the far wall, Bridget didn't know how he got anything done. Several times, he took a small pad out of his shirt pocket and wrote notes telling the person on the other side of the line he'd have to look and get back to them.

"That ain't no fun." Lizzy pouted, looking up at Luke with the biggest blue eyes Bridget had ever seen. The little girl's dark hair lay plaited in two sweet braids on either side of her head. The only thing more adorable would have been two ribbon bows, which made Bridget think of the small stash she kept in the top drawer of her dresser with scraps of ribbon and fabric.

"It is when it's a treasure hunt." Luke winked at Bridget as he hunched down beside Lizzy. "Some of these things are Miss Bridget's, but I think I might have hit the mother-load behind the shopping center."

"Uncle Luke." Lizzy rolled her eyes. "Momma told you it ain't sanitary to dive in them dumper things."

Luke tugged on one of Lizzy's braids. "And she also told you 'ain't' isn't a word."

Bridget laughed. She couldn't help herself. Luke tilted his head and looked up at her. She placed her hand over her mouth. Lizzy glanced between the two and grinned. Before she knew it, Lizzy jumped to her feet and grabbed Bridget's hand. "Come then, a treasure-hunting we go."

Behind Luke's truck, Lizzy let go of Bridget long enough for Luke to lift Lizzy onto the tailgate.

"I take it you two do this often?" Bridget waited, clasping her hands in front of her, feeling awkward standing at the truck's tailgate. Her broken dresser wouldn't fit in the RV. She didn't know what she'd do with it.

"Lisa works in town at the bank. She leaves the girls here with me or sometimes with the Shaws on days I have got places to go," Luke said.

"Daddy's fighting the bad people." Lizzy sat down on the tailgate of the truck, her feet swinging.

"Is he?" Bridget asked.

Lizzy nodded. "Yep. There's a lot of bad people."

"Lizzy …" Luke said.

"Yes, there is." Bridget rocked back and forth from toe to heel.

"That's not what she means." Luke patted Lizzy and pointed to a box behind her. "Doug is overseas."

"I've never met my daddy." Lizzy crawled on her knees to pull the box forward. "But I write him letters."

"You do?" Bridget looked between Luke and Lizzy.

"Yep. My granny writes them, and I put pictures in with them."

"I bet he cherishes them."

"Alright, Lizzy girl. Let's get this stuff off and see what goodies we find in here." Luke took the box and headed into the barn.

"Oh, Uncle Luke. Can't we show Brig It the goats? I want to play with the goats."

Luke returned and rolled his eyes. "Always find a way to get out of work. Go on then, show Miss Bridget the goats."

"Yay!" Lizzy hopped off the truck and grabbed Bridget by the hand. "Come on."

Pulled by Lizzy, Bridget stumbled along. The little girl released her, running into the barn. Bridget walked after her.

"Uncle Luke, the fence!"

"I got it, pumpkin." Luke chuckled. He winked at Bridget as Lizzy came running back out. Grabbing Bridget by the hand, Lizzy took her behind the barn. A dozen goats grazed in the field.

"Unhook it." Lizzy pointed to the bright yellow handle holding the wire across the posts.

Bridget reached for the handle.

"Zap!" Lizzy shouted.

Bridget jumped and screamed, her hand on her heart.

Lizzy squealed in laughter.

Luke sprinted around the corner. "What happened?"

"That was not nice!" Bridget fought to restore her heart in her chest. The girl sensed her nervousness around the electric fence.

"You should have seen her face, Uncle Luke!"

"Lizzy." Luke looked sternly at the little girl. "Miss Bridget is from the city. It's not nice to scare her like that."

Lizzy made a face. "I'm sorry, Brig It."

Bridget thought it cut the way Lizzy said her name. The girl made her smile with her cuteness. "Goats, huh?"

"They eat the weeds around the junk." Luke took hold of the handle and let down the wire. "You can leave this down until you're done."

"Don't you worry about the goats will get out?"

Lizzy walked out ahead of them toward a group of three white and brown goats.

"They do anyway. Lisa gets mad when they cross the road and go into the yard. "

"And those?" Bridget nodded to the horses she'd spotted earlier in the morning.

"Misty and Romeo. They're Lisa and Doug's horses. They're in the other section away from the salvage field, they can't get over here."

"Come on, Brig It, meet Lumpy." Lizzy hugged the neck of a very chubby goat with a brown head. The little goat appeared like it swallowed a watermelon and bayed at her.

"I don't do goats." Bridget winced, watching Lizzy stand and pet the goat. Another goat pushed into the little girl. Lizzy turned and gave the other goat attention.

"We've got a cat in the barn." His eyes had this gleam. She couldn't help noticing.

"We never had pets. They were never allowed."

"Sounds like you need to stay in the country a while."

Bridget's heart did a little skip. Lizzy yelled and motioned for her to come. Bridget walked out toward the goats. Luke waved as he turned and headed up to the front of the barn.

"You can pet Flip Flop," Lizzy said.

Bridget paused. The goats didn't pay her much mind, but the one Lizzy called Flip Flop started walking towards her, and Bridget froze. "They're just like dogs, right?"

Lizzy giggled. "They don't bark."

Flip Flop came up to Bridget. The little brown and white goat dipped its head to graze.

"Go on. Pet her."

Slowly, Bridget reached out and laid her hand on the goat. Surprised to find the goat's hair soft, she ran her hand down the goat's head and neck.

"See, it's not so bad."

Looking out over the salvaged junk in the field toward the two horses grazing on the hill, Bridget prayed, *Lord, what have I gotten myself into?*

5

When Lisa came home, Luke returned Lizzy to her mother. Inside the kitchen, she stacked groceries on the counter. "I couldn't take two steps down the vegetable aisle before having someone ask me questions about my 'house guest.'"

"Only one knows she's here, is you." Luke didn't bother trying to grab anything from the fridge. He moved out of his sister's way. She slammed a cupboard door shut, giving a wicked stare and going on about putting the rest of her groceries away.

"I made it clear she was staying in Dad's old RV, and you'd be taking her back where she belongs before long. Like yesterday."

Angie peered around the corner. "Momma, can we watch TV?"

Lisa turned and put on a smile for her daughter. "Just until supper." Then she looked at Luke. "You eating with us tonight?"

"You extending the invite?" Luke crossed his arms.

"Since when we got to invite Uncle Luke to supper?" Angie asked.

"We don't." Lisa walked over and kissed the little girl on top of the head.

"You gonna bring Bridget, too?"

Luke uncrossed his arms. "Not tonight. I've got a hankering for a burger down at the diner."

Lisa snorted. "Don't forget to bring in the horses before you leave."

Luke tipped back his ball cap. Little Lizzy came around the corner. "Can I come?"

"You'd best stay with your momma," Luke said. "I think she might have missed you."

Lisa reached in a bag pulling out a jar of pickles. "Here you go. Put this in the pantry."

"Don't forget to give Romeo a carrot." Lizzy danced away with the pickles.

Luke walked up close to Lisa. "We could sell the horses. All you have to do is say the word."

And Lisa's face drained of color. She folded the empty bag and reached for another. "I can't. You know that."

Luke nodded. "Then I suppose you won't mind if I take our guest for a ride this evening since you know she'll be staying with us a while, and those horses could use a little attention now and again."

Liza scowled at him. "We're short at the bank. Mariah Gilbert is out on maternity."

"I know it." Luke headed out of the door.

Lizzy rushed up and slapped a carrot in his hand. "You almost forgot."

"Good thing I've got you." Luke ran his hand down the side of the child's face as he left the house. Outside he took a deep fresh breath of air and said a prayer for his sister's heart.

Walking across the road, he spied Bridget sitting outside the RV beside an old lawn chair. Tangled in baler twine, she didn't seem to notice him until he stood beside the chair.

She braided, twisted, and knotted the twine between the metal frame. "I'm sorry I broke it, but I can fix it."

"Was it the one by the RV?" he asked.

"No, I found it by the barn."

He didn't know how she figured out which piece of twine to twist and weave next. "It was probably broken before you sat in it. There's a few more up by the old shed behind the house if you want to string and knot those, too."

She laughed. "It's called macrame. Don't tell me you never learned how to make knots and twist twine, farm boy?"

"Nope." Luke couldn't say he had. "I spent my time helping on the farm, mostly fixing things. Always something breaking around here."

She wrapped the twine around the metal and tied another knot. Glancing at him, she looked thoughtful, then sad. He'd seen that look on his sister a time or two.

"Looks like it might storm tonight. I'm headed out to bring in the horses. I thought you might give me a hand."

"The horses out in the field?"

"Those would be the ones," he said.

"I don't do horses." She resumed braiding the twine.

"Lizzy sent a carrot. Come on, I'll let you lead the gelding. He's got a good head on him." He wouldn't take no for an answer. He held his hand out to her. She pressed her lips together. Sighing, she reached her hand up, and he placed the carrot in her hand. "I'll get the lead rope."

He turned away to hide his amusement at her shocked face. When he returned from grabbing the leads in the barn, he found her finishing up her ties on the edge of the lawn chair seat. "Ready?"

She fell into step alongside him. He spied the carrot in her back pocket. "I'm not sure this is a good idea."

"You ever been close to a horse?" He opened the gate for her into the pasture.

"There are a few in the city, mostly police horses." She kept her distance, a step behind him. Luke adjusted his stride to keep her at his side. "Not that I've ever been in trouble with the police, mind you. Because I haven't. Ever been arrested, that is."

He handed her a red nylon lead strap, his fingers brushing against hers as she took it. "I have."

She did a double-take, and it made him smile.

"What?"

"I was a teenager; a few buddies and I went out looking for something to do one night. Old man, Thompson left his tractor out in the field. We thought it'd be funny to move the tractor, you know, put it in a different field up the road further."

He didn't know if her face turned to appalled or amused. Both her slender brows rose.

"What happened?"

Several of the goats had spotted them and started walking toward them. Luke steered her around an old plow toward the second strand of the fence between the two pastures. "The tractor sat on a hill, it flipped, and one of us had to go for help."

Bridget gasped. "Oh, that is terrible."

"Yeah, it was. Tyler lucked out with a broken leg and a few broken ribs. While Pete and I got charged with attempted theft."

"Ouch." She twisted the lead around her hand.

"Not as painful as having to work off the debt of paying for a new tractor." Luke opened the gate for her. "I spent the entire rest of my junior year in school milking old man Thompson's cows before and after school."

"At least you didn't go to jail."

"No. If it hadn't been for old man Thompson, I wouldn't have had my chance in the major leagues."

He could see she wanted to ask him something, but the

goats caught up with him. A tall black and white speckled goat nipped at her back pocket. Bridget jumped to the side.

"It's after the carrot." He chuckled.

"Oh no, you don't." Bridget pulled the carrot out and tried to hand it to Luke.

He kept the goats at bay while Bridget slipped past the gate into the horse pasture. The brown and white goat from earlier cried out in protest.

"Here." She handed him the carrot. "You give it to them."

He broke it in half and handed her the other half. "You'll need this. Otherwise, Romeo won't let you get near him."

At the sound of his name, the horse raised his head.

"Yeah." Bridget looked out at the horses. "I think I'll stay here. You bring them in all the time, right? You don't need me."

Luke pressed his hand against the small of her back. "How are you ever gonna ride one if you don't even get to know them first?"

Bridget froze. "Ride them? Oh, no." She waved her hand. "I don't do horses. I told you. City girl. We walk on our own two feet or ride these things called bicycles. No horses."

"That is what you say." Luke took her hand and tugged at it.

"Oh. I know."

He could feel the fear radiating in her grip on his hand. "Relax." He gave her fingers an extra squeeze. "They can sense your fear."

"Is this where you tell me they are more afraid of me than I am of them?"

"Nope." Luke laughed, and he felt her stiffen beside him. Lisa's horse, Misty, a high-strung sorrel thoroughbred, had walked towards him.

"Don't move," he said.

Misty shook her head up and down as she approached. Her lips twitched out. Luke held out his half of the carrot.

Bridget stiffened at his side. He spoke calmly to the horse, drawing the horse closer and hoping to reassure the woman beside him. "Hey, girl. Storm's coming. What do you say we head in, bed down for the night?"

Misty nickered in response. The mare chomped down on the carrot in Luke's hand. He reached up and took the horse by the halter. He ran his hand down her thin white blaze. "Good girl."

He snapped the lead under the halter.

Bridget stepped away from him, Romeo a few inches taller at the wither than Misty had grown curious and come trotting towards them. "Hold out the carrot. Flat on your palm. Keep your fingers together."

The chestnut gelding slowed to a walk. Bridget twisted and held her hand with the carrot. Her face turned away. Luke kept a tight hold on Misty to keep the mare from snatching the gelding's treat.

"Please don't bite me. Please don't bite me," she muttered.

Romeo stopped short of her hand.

Luke stepped behind her and slid his hand beneath hers. A pleasant tingle glided over his fingertips as he guided her hand toward the horse. "Relax."

Romeo stretched his neck and nibbled at the carrot. Then the horse stepped up and finished taking the carrot from her. Her big and broad smile caused a warmth in his chest. He almost forgot about Misty until the mare bumped into him.

"Don't forget the lead." Luke held Misty away. "Take hold of his halter, then snap the lead on the metal ring underneath."

Bridget reached over, took hold of the side of the navy halter, and reached with the lead. "Easy, boy. Just gonna clip this. Right here."

She clipped the lead under his halter. "I did it."

"You give him a carrot. He'll be your best friend forever."

Luke winked. He reached over and slid his hand down the mare's blaze.

"And you?" Bridget ducked her head, but he caught the hint of pink in her cheeks. He wondered if she knew how cute she looked, flirting with him. A rumble from the sky above reminded him of their purpose, and Luke cleared his throat. "We'd best get these two back to the barn before the rain comes."

"Of course." Bridget waved her hand, and Romeo jerked away. She cringed. "Sorry."

"No sudden movements."

"No sudden movements. Got it." She repeated, following him as they led the horses to the barn.

6

Bridget counted the money in her wallet down to the penny, thirty-seven dollars, and sixty-two cents. She'd always been one to take care of herself. With this much, she'd become a burden to him sooner rather than later. Which in her book, said she needed to get out of here sooner rather than later. She liked Luke. More than she had a right. She needed to get out of this blink of a town.

"Whatcha doing?" Lizzy stood in the doorway.

Bridget looked up from packing her black satchel. She stuffed the last of the order forms in the pocket. "Getting ready to get to work."

Lizzy's little lips formed an O. "You got a job?"

Silly as it sounded coming from the mouth of a three-year-old, Bridget almost laughed. She clipped the flap shut and stood up from her kneeling position. Hitching the bag's strap over her shoulder, she said, "Sort of."

She wouldn't lie to the little girl. She'd been selling junk merchandise out of her bag for over a year. Only a few months ago, the company had gone belly up, leaving her with what she had left in her bag.

"Like what?" Lizzy asked.

Bridget looked down at the little girl. So innocent ... so sweet.

"Selling stuff." She walked past the little girl and out of the building Luke often referred to as his machine shed. It comprised large square paned windows covered in dirt; everywhere she looked was a metal heap or junk pile. She hadn't quite decided yet if Luke Myers was a Mr. Fix-It or some kind of artist by the looks of the contraptions sitting around this place.

"There's lots of stuff to sell here." Lizzy spread her arms open to show Bridget all the stuff in the shed.

"Looks like a scrap heap to me," Bridget said.

Lizzy frowned. "Uncle Luke says that one man's junk is another man's treasure."

She bent down level with Luke's niece. "He's got you brainwashed, doesn't he? Listen, sweetie. Junk is garbage people throw away. It's not meant for people to salvage."

"But he picked you up. I heard my momma say so."

Bridget sucked in her breath. She couldn't help wondering what else Luke's sister had told her daughters where Bridget was concerned. It didn't matter. She would be gone in a few days. Giving Lizzy her best smile, the one she practiced for drawing in potential customers, she tweaked Lizzy's nose with her finger. "Lucky me."

Lizzy followed her out and around the corner of the shed. Luke held a blowtorch in one hand and flipped up his protective face mask with the other. Sitting a safe distance away with a coloring book and crayons spread out on a blanket, Angie glanced over at them.

Turning off the gas, the torch went out. "Where are you goin'?"

"She's going to sell stuff," Lizzy said.

Bridget tilted up her chin. "It's not that I don't appreciate everything you've done for me, but I've got to make my own way, you know."

Luke's eyes narrowed on her. He laid down the torch and took off his mask.

Lizzy grabbed hold of her hand. "Can I go? Can I? Please?"

"I'm afraid you'll have to stay here with your uncle. Besides, I'm sure your mother wouldn't like it if she found you with me."

Pools of tears gathered in Lizzy's eyes, but before they could spill, Luke swept her up into his arms. She squirmed and giggled as he tickled her. "Don't like your Uncle Luke anymore?"

"No! No!" Lizzy screamed between giggles.

Luke kissed the little girl's forehead and set her down on her feet again. "You stay here with me, kid."

"But, I want to go with Brig It." Lizzy pouted.

"Sometimes we got to let people do things on their own," Luke looked at Bridget. She felt her face flush and ducked her head.

"But why?" Lizzy asked.

"Do you like it when Angie pours your milk, and you can do it yourself?" Luke asked.

Lizzy shook her head.

"Why don't you go over with Angie? I think your momma needs some new pictures for on her fridge," Luke said.

Lizzy's eyes lit up. "And Brig-It. She needs one too!"

"I can't wait." Bridget walked away, but Luke stepped in front of her.

"The people here are good folk. It's a small town."

She looked up, gazing into his eyes, swallowing hard. Slowly, he stepped out of her way. "If you wait until I finish welding this frame, I can drive you into town."

"It can't be that far. I can walk. I am used to walking everywhere," she scuffed.

Luke reached into his pocket and pulled out a little flip phone. "If you find you can't walk back, call. The number is listed as 'barn' to reach me here. You'll find it out in the shed."

"That's kind of you, but I'm a big girl. It's a straight walk down the road into town. I think I can manage." She couldn't bring herself to accept it.

"I'm sure you can but take the phone, anyway." Luke took her hand and pressed the phone in her palm.

"What if someone calls you?" She held it out to him.

Luke shrugged. "Answer it. However, it doesn't work until you get closer to town. Service can be spotty in these parts."

About to argue, the rigid set of Luke's jaw caused her to accept the phone. She placed his phone in her bag and pulled away from him. No one ever cared if she got lost or needed help. An unfamiliar feeling gave her a pleasant sense of security. Heading for the road, her throat tightened, and her fingers trembled a little.

As she got to the end of the lane, Lizzy shouted and waved. Bridget couldn't help waving in return.

Setting into a leisurely paced walk, she glanced over her shoulder to see the barn and junk far behind her. Bridget allowed hope to bloom. Not a lot, because she'd been down that road too many times, but a little. Small town or not, she'd find a way to return to the city and stand on her own two feet again. God willing.

Usually, she would have been like a kid grabbing a cookie out of the cookie jar before dinner, but once she reached the town, she hadn't stopped at one house along the way. What was wrong with her?

This was a new town. New people. A fresh start.

Her feet aching, she slumped on a bench outside a funeral home after she passed the post office. She slid the strap of her satchel from her shoulder and left the bag to fall to her side. Nothing inside added to the reflection of worth she had seen in Luke's eyes earlier. If only for a moment, she could look at herself through his eyes and see what he saw. She sighed as a car pulled up, parking at the curb. She watched as an older gentleman got out and went around to the other side. He opened the door and assisted a woman to the sidewalk.

The woman sobbed, and the man wrapped his arm around her. Bridget reached into her bag, tossing item after item onto the bench until she found a lace hankie. Jumping to her feet, she held a picture frame still clutched in her other hand.

The man scowled at her, and the woman paused with a shocked expression on her face. Realizing her mistake, Bridget switched outstretched hands, offering the woman the hankie.

Quickly the couple rushed into the funeral home, leaving her standing on the sidewalk. Slowly, she lowered her arm.

From behind, she heard a sound and turned. A family walked by her, brushing against her shoulder and pushing her back a step. She slumped down onto the bench. As she picked up the items from her bag, she bumped a light-up keychain on the sidewalk.

"Here, let me get that." Bridget looked over to watch a woman bend and pick up the key chain. Her kind smile reached clear to her warm brown eyes. Her wheat-toned hair was pulled up in a messy bun. She didn't appear much older than Bridget, probably in her late twenties.

"Thanks," Bridget mumbled, taking the key chain and stuffing it into her bag.

"That there is one of those sales rep kits, isn't it?" the woman asked.

"Our youth sold those last year. Didn't the company go out of business?"

"Yeah, about six months ago," Bridget said.

"Trying to sell off the last of stock. I don't blame you. My name is Anne, by the way. I own the beauty shop down the street. The one with the purple trim around the door." Anne laughed as if she'd made a joke and smiled at Bridget. "It's the only one in town."

"Bridget." She hitched her satchel strap over her shoulder.

Anne regarded her for a moment. "You're the woman Luke picked up and brought back to the farm."

It shouldn't be any surprise to her, a small town. The word probably spread like wildfire around a small town like Hidden Hills.

"I didn't mean it that way. I planned on grabbing some coffee at the diner after paying my respects. Why don't you meet me there? It looks like we could both use a friend today."

At the mention of friends, Bridget winced. Shelby had been her friend, and look where it got her. Besides Luke bringing her to this little blink of a town, the only other person she had to talk to was Lizzy. It would be nice to have a conversation with someone closer to her age, and Anne might be a valuable connection to helping her find her way around town.

Bridget chewed on her lip. More people headed down the street toward them, and traffic had picked up through town since she'd first started sitting there.

Anne smiled, and Bridget shrugged. "Sure. Why not?"

"I'll just be a moment. Mrs. Wagner passed on a few nights ago. Precious woman, always came in every week for her wash and set," Anne reached up to dab away a few tears.

Not knowing what else to say or do, Bridget pointed to the diner. "I'll just meet you there."

Anne's smile reappeared. "I won't be long."

Bridget watched as the woman rushed away into the funeral home. She turned away, stuffing the album and hankie back in her case. Another car went by, and Bridget crossed the street.

Overhead the bell rang as she entered the little diner. There were a few patrons at a table near the window. Bridget took a seat where she could look across to the funeral home. Part of her waited, while the other part told her that Anne wouldn't show up.

"What can I get you?"

Bridget looked up at the portly waitress. She held a pot of coffee in one hand and her fist on her hip with the other.

"Just coffee."

The waitress flipped over a mug in front of her and poured the steaming black liquid.

Bridget hitched her satchel around the back of the chair and watched out the window. Several more people entered the funeral home.

"Died in her sleep, she did, and all alone," the waitress clucked her tongue and moved behind the counter.

There were creamers and sugar on the table in a little tray by the window, and Bridget grabbed two of each. She kept her eye on the funeral home. Wrapping her hands around the warm cup and sipping as she waited. Half a cup later, Anne emerged from the funeral home. Bridget heard the little bell above the door chime as the other woman entered the diner and joined her.

"Sorry it took so long. I ran into Marge. I wanted to compliment her on all the nice floral arrangements she did for Ruth. She always loved yellow roses, and often I'd put one in her hair for special occasions." Anne took out a tissue and wiped the dampness from her eyes.

"Anne." The waitress acknowledged. "Coffee for you, too?"

"Oh yes, Gwen, thank you." Anne turned and smiled at Bridget. "So, where are you from?"

Bridget snorted, taking a sip of her coffee. Nobody had ever asked. Usually, the question concerned where she was going, not where she had been. A lot of places, some she'd rather forget, crossed her mind as she looked at Anne.

"I was born in Lexington," Bridget said.

"I've always been here in Hidden Hills," Anne said.

"Must have been nice," Bridget muttered, trying to smile and be polite.

But if Anne heard the bitterness in her voice, she paid it no mind. "I can't imagine being anywhere else. Mrs. Wagner taught at the school in the church until it closed a few years ago. She retired, but I remember her as my first-grade teacher."

Bridget took another sip of her coffee. People came and went inside the funeral home across the street.

"My cousin Rebecca used to date Luke in high school," Anne said.

Bridget looked at the other woman, unsure where that remark had come from. Anne swept a piece of wheat-toned hair behind her shoulder and gazed out the window. "The whole town was so proud of him when he went to Louisville to play baseball. A few of us even took a trip to see him play."

Bridget vaguely remembered him mentioning playing ball. "I didn't know."

Gwen came and topped off their coffee. She lingered a bit, fussing with the sugars. A little clear gem winked from her blue and red painted nails. "I'll be back again real soon if you need anything."

From the looks inside the little diner, Gwen would check on them often. Only two other tables had customers and smells of grilled burgers and cheese drifted through the tables.

"People get excited around here, small-town folk making it big. Shame, Luke quit after his dad passed," Anne said wistfully.

Poor Luke. She'd been there. Done that sort of thing. If her grandmother had just held on a while longer, she might not have ended up like this — living in an RV, in a strange town, with no way out. That's how she'd felt when she'd faced choosing between her career and sitting by her dying grandmother's side.

How awful for Luke.

"We all thought he'd be somebody." Anne took a sip of her coffee.

Bridget sat down with her cup and stared at Anne. "Be somebody? Like he isn't somebody now?"

"Oh, I didn't mean it like that." Anne waved off Bridget's reaction.

Anne didn't mean a lot of things. Bridget tilted her head and watched Anne take another sip of coffee.

"Luke's been a real blessing to the community. He may not have become the famous ballplayer we all expected of him, but he coaches those boys on the baseball field, and they think the world of him. Everyone thought he'd hook up with Jimmy Weston's mother, Sonya. And then he brought you home."

"Oh, no! It's not like that!"

Anne placed her hand on Bridget's before she jumped out of her seat. "I didn't say it was. Luke's momma taught him right. He's a good man. A man who cares about family and taking care of others. When he came back, and his momma went to the nursing home, Luke lived in that old RV while he remodeled the basement of his parent's house. He gave Lisa and the girls the main floor when they needed a place to live."

"I see." Bridget shifted in her seat. She didn't feel right hearing these things about Luke. As good as they were, they should come from getting to know him and not from the local gossip. They were on a need-to-know basis, but she couldn't help being curious about a man who would pick up trash off the streets and give up a professional career as an athlete.

Anne motioned for Gwen to come over. "We'll have a slice of that pie Ben baked this morning. The apple, I think. It's on me," Anne said before Bridget could protest.

Bridget bit her lip and nodded. While Gwen went off to fetch the pie, Anne leaned forward on her elbows. The coffee mug sat between her arms. "I tell you these things because they're important for someone coming in from the outside to know. You're staying in the old RV Luke's dad traded John Beck for before he died. He planned to take Darla, Luke's

mother, on a few trips, but it didn't happen. After Harry
Myers passed, Luke took over his dad's salvage business and
fixin' things the way he always did. If he had a junk car, and
Harry could fix it, he'd see the person who needed it get it.
Luke's a lot like his dad. He knows, and the good Lord knows
it too because He brought you here."

Bridget had never felt more grateful for pie than when
Gwen came up behind Anne and placed the two plates in
front of them. Hesitant, Bridget didn't like to take handouts
from others. Her granny would object, saying to take what the
good Lord offered and be blessed, but right now, Bridget
didn't feel blessed. She felt obligated to Luke and this woman.
And she didn't like those feelings at all.

"I don't suppose you need any help over at your shop," she
asked, praying to change the subject.

Anne shook her head. "I wish I did. If you're looking for
work, you're best off going to Shelbyville or even Hatton. A
lot of people commute from here."

Bridget sighed.

"Looks like someone's come looking for you." Anne
pointed out the window. Bridget didn't miss the twinkle in
Anne's eye.

Luke's blue pickup drove down the street.

Anne left a few bills on the table, and they walked outside
the diner. A moment later, Luke and the girls came around
and pulled up against the curb. He reached over and pushed
open the door for her.

"You stop in at the salon and visit anytime, you hear? It
was nice meeting you."

Bridget waved as Anne walked away. Gwen, the waitress,
came out onto the street. "Give these here to Luke and be
careful. You don't want to be spilling the gravy."

Walking up to the truck, Bridget saw Luke grinning at her.
"Lizzy got hungry. You heading back?"

"Looks like I am now." She scooted in beside Angie. "Your uncle doesn't cook, does he?"

Angie shook her head.

"And here I thought he could do everything."

Both the girls giggled as Luke scowled.

7

Luke swore and shook his finger as he nicked it on the sharp edge of a gear. He dropped his ratchet. It fell inside the hollow crankshaft he'd been working on all morning. He wiped his smarting finger on his pants, not about to suck on the throbbing digit with grease smeared over it.

As he had the past several mornings, he looked for her, annoyed more with himself for caring then how she took off to town each day. Luke stood, forgot about the ratchet, and pulled a grease rag from his rear pocket. He spotted her, squinting against the afternoon sun. She walked down the side of the road.

He'd grin now while she couldn't see him. Luke wiped his fingers, pocketed the rag again, and hunched beside the motor. He wouldn't let her see him watching her come down the drive or cross the gravel parking area by the barn. But, when he sensed her near, he dared a look.

She wore a maxi skirt with a pair of white canvas shoes. He caught the navy color of her hem as she passed. "Lunch is on the table by the door."

She paused; her bewildered expression stirred something in him. "You made me lunch?"

He needed to fish his ratchet out of the motor. "You eat, don't you?"

"How did you know I'd be back?" She approached him, blocked the sun, and created a moment of shade. A breeze fluttered through, rustling a few leaves, picking up the tip of his tarp beneath the motor. Amongst the heady scent of gasoline, motor oil, and his sweat, he smelled her — sweet like the surrounding breeze. Her scent reminded him of fresh linens on the line and pumpkin pie.

She must have walked by the diner or taken a shortcut through Snyder's pumpkin patch.

"It wasn't hard to guess. You left your stuff here. I don't figure you'd leave without it." Quiet, he glanced at her. She gave him a look, and he realized that wasn't what she'd meant, but it had been what hung in his mind all morning.

"Thank you," she said so quietly he couldn't be sure he'd heard her. She retreated to the old milk house. After he got his ratchet and put his tools away, he joined her. She'd polished off the sandwich he had made for her and made quicker work of the chips — not leaving him one. But she surprised him by sliding her can of soda in his direction.

"Surely, you're thirsty."

"I'd prefer a water, if I may?" she asked.

He walked to the little fridge he kept in the milk house, got her out a bottle of water, and placed it in front of her. "You can help yourself to what's in the fridge."

"Why are you doing this?" she asked.

He waited for her to drink and pushed the bottle closer. "It's water. That's what you asked for, isn't it?'

"I suppose I owe you." She stared at the bottle, her hand resting on the cap.

What was it with women these days? Always thinking they had to pay a man back!

"We don't charge for water in these parts."

She laughed. A giddy sound he liked. He wished he could

make her laugh more — realized he wanted to. He'd make her laugh so hard the tears he saw just behind her eyes would come because of joy.

He'd heard her the night before through his open window. She sobbed, and it untied so many knots in his chest he'd worked up during the years. He didn't know a woman's sorrows could loosen a man like that. Or him, like it did.

While she drank, he went around the barn and pulled out the vintage bicycle with the metal basket. He'd spent the better part of his morning replacing the chain, fixing the breaks, and searching for a basket the right size. He'd found an old wire basket inside a deep freezer and fixed it upright to fit across the handlebars for her.

He wheeled it over by the doorway, and when she looked up at him, questioning, he couldn't stop the swell of pride in his chest. "It's not much, but two wheels to get to town and back are better than none."

He would have taken her if she asked him. He didn't know why women in the city had to go about thinking they needed to be independent and self-reliant. While the farm layout the road close to town, it still took a man a good hour or more to walk there, not to mention a woman with short legs. He'd have saddled up one of the horses if he didn't think Lisa would have such a fit, but a bicycle seemed more practical. And by the look on Bridget's face, he couldn't say whether or not she liked it.

"You can ride a bicycle, can't you? You mentioned people riding them in the city, I figured you'd know how to use one."

Bridget got up and came closer to the bicycle. She ran her hand over the white frame, dotted with rust here and there. She didn't say a word, and he couldn't see her face. "They say that riding a bike is like riding a horse. You never forget how."

She glanced over at him, a smile playing on her lips, but the glaze of her watery eyes caused his heart to pick up speed. "I know how."

"I can adjust the seat if it's too high." He placed his hand over hers on the handlebars. She blinked several times, biting her lip. She glanced away from him to where his hand lay atop hers. "Thank you."

"It's just a bike." He pulled his hand away, heat creeping up his neck. "I didn't figure you had a driver's license or if you do, I can find you a car and fix it up."

Her eyes lifted to his. It pulled at his gut, making him step closer to her.

"I have never needed one. The bicycle is fine. It's great. I'll pay you back."

"I pulled it from some junk up in the field. You don't owe me anything for it."

"But if it's here, then it's your property. I'll pay you for it," she insisted.

"Usually, people pay me to take their junk. Consider it a favor." And he meant it.

In a blur, she popped up on her tippy toes and smacked his cheek with a quick kiss. She darted off with the bicycle toward the RV, leaving him too embarrassed to touch the spot her lips had been. He cleared his throat, heading toward the old milk house to grab his unfinished soda, whistling a tune as he went.

By Saturday, they'd fallen into a routine. Luke watched Bridget pace around the machine shed. Inside the old milk house off the side of the barn, she spied the old Pentium computer and had spent many hours staring at the screen. He never could find much interest in going online, but it appeared to fill a void in her day.

He'd almost finished with the washing machine when he heard a truck pull up in front of the shed doors. He cleaned his hands and opened the door.

"I came by to see if you could use any of this junk on the back of the ole pickup."

Luke stepped outside. He spotted Bridget looking up at him from sorting a pile of discarded fabrics. He'd told her she didn't have to do that, but he didn't argue when she complained she needed to do something.

He looked at the pile of old appliances and a few strips of house gutters dangling over the bed of the pickup. He spotted an antique wringer washer and pointed it out. "I think that one has some potential."

From the corner of his eye, he spotted Bridget leaning against the doorjamb, watching them.

"I thought that might interest you," Pete Patterson said. He pulled down the tailgate of the truck and climbed up. Luke and Pete went back through their high school days.

"Ever do anything with that stove I brought you?" Pete pushed the washer closer to the tailgate.

"Come on in and see for yourself," Luke said.

Bridget pushed up the shed door, carrying the ringer washer inside.

"I'll be. You took that scrap and made something out of it?" Pete pulled out a handkerchief and wiped the sweat from his brow.

Bridget resumed sorting, pretending not to watch them, but Luke could feel her curious stare on his back. Pete followed his gaze. "Anne said you had someone staying here."

"Just until she can find a place and get back on her feet." Or at least that had been what he told himself.

Pete didn't look so convinced. "Always knew you'd come home one day with a girl; just didn't think you'd be the type to pick one up off the street."

Luke's jaw tightened. He felt his fist clench and took a deep breath to let it go. He pulled the sheet off the stove and changed the subject. "Took a while, but finally came up with a design that worked."

Pete rocked on the heels of his boots and whistled low. "Now that's a man's grill if I ever saw one."

Both men seemed content to allow the subject of Bridget to drop.

The oven of the stainless-steel gas stove had worked, so Luke hooked it up to a propane tank. He'd replaced the burners with a grill top and extended two fold-out burners on either side. He'd painted the grill part red and the knobs black.

"If you want it. It's yours," Luke said.

Pete's expression changed from surprise to total disagreement. "No. I couldn't."

"Think of the barbecues you could have on Sundays after church," Luke said.

Pete took another look at the grill. He and his wife threw a barbecue every Sunday in the summer for the members of their church.

"I don't have room for it just now," Pete said.

"Just stop by on your way back through later. I'll help you load it."

Pete clamped Luke by the hand. "Thanks, man."

Luke walked him out to the truck.

"You be careful now. Never know what you can pick up out there at the city dumpsters."

Luke knew Pete meant well, but his friend's words put a splinter under his skin. How many other folks would think that? How many of them had his sister tainted?

Luke glanced up at the sky and to the heavens, saying a quick prayer for his sister and Bridget.

Not long after Pete drove away, Luke sensed someone standing beside him in the parking lot. Glancing over, his heart squeezed at the sight of Bridget. A breeze stirred and blew strands of her hair against her face.

She didn't show it if she had heard the things Pete had said.

"You could have sold that, you know."

"I know." He walked into the garage. Pete may have been right. The first time he brought a girl home to the farm. It seemed right. Bridget felt right here.

She followed him. "Do you always give away everything you make?"

"Not always."

She gazed at him, crossing her arms and watching him pull the sheet back over the grill. He knew Pete would come before noon to pick it up.

"I wouldn't have given it away," she mumbled. "Person could make a good living selling stuff like that."

"Think so?"

She shrugged. "How many other things you got?"

"It's all in there." He pointed toward the back corner of the shed, and her expression changed. An idea struck him.

"So that's what all this junk is. I just figured it was furniture or something."

"It is, or some of it."

One by one, he pulled off the sheets of his creations. Tables, chairs, washers, stoves, and lamps lined up across every shed wall.

"You could sell this."

"Go ahead," he knew she hadn't had any luck selling her merchandise in town or finding a job.

"Serious? You want me to sell your stuff?" She tilted her head and looked at him.

"I suppose we could work out some sort of commission. But this isn't the Galleria, you know."

Her face lit up as she turned around, gazing at all the items he'd made. Most of which had been things he'd picked up from places and restored or recreated with parts from something else.

She walked through the shed, touching a finger to the dirt

on the surfaces and studying each piece for a moment at a time. Finally, she turned to him. "Fifteen percent."

"Fifty."

"Twenty," she said.

"Forty-five."

"Thirty."

"Deal." He held out his hand to her, and she took it. He chuckled at the bewildered look on her face. He reached out, wanting to pull her in and kiss that adorable look on her face, when he stopped. She took his hand as if he offered it to shake. His fingers curled around her slender ones and shook on them.

8

Bridget spent the night making a list of all Luke's items and researching them on the internet for something comparable in price. She wrote up a plan, starting with cleaning up an area in the shed for a showroom. For the first time since her grand-mother's death, she felt the vigor of having a purpose again.

She smelled coffee in the morning and found Lizzy and Angie racing around the shed in matching plaid skirts and black cardigans.

Pouring herself a cup, she spotted Luke coming across the road from the basement entrance of the house. She frowned over the steam of her coffee. He wore a pair of slacks and a button-down shirt and had traded his tattered ball cap for a Stetson.

A little flutter swirled in her stomach. He didn't look bad all dressed up, especially with that cowboy hat tilted low. "What's the occasion?"

"It's Sunday!" Angie said, chasing Lizzy around a table.

"You still have about a half-hour to get ready," Luke said.

Bridget choked on her coffee. "You mean church?" Her chest clogged, and her lungs felt like they had a wrench stuck in them.

Lizzy raced around and grabbed hold of her. "You can sit with me."

Angie's hand shot out and tried to grab Lizzy from around Bridget. "Maybe she doesn't want to go with us."

Bridget sat down her coffee before she spilled the hot liquid on herself or one of the girls.

"I suppose ..." Bridget said.

"It's not a problem, is it?" Luke asked. He walked up beside her and shooed away the girls.

"No. It's just that ..." How could she tell him she'd longed to be back in a church community? After losing her grandmother, she'd lost her job and apartment and been forced to jump from roommate to roommate. None of them had shared her same beliefs.

But the years had hardened her.

Lizzy screamed, and Angie cried. Both she and Luke turned at the sound of a crash behind them. Angie sat on the floor, holding the hem of her cardigan and crying.

Luke rushed over, and Bridget followed. Lizzy stood, her eyes wide. "I didn't mean to."

Bridget held her breath.

"It's okay, as long as no one is hurt." Luke bent down where Angie sat. "You okay?"

"I ripped my sweater," Angie cried.

"Momma's gonna be mad at you," Lizzy said.

As Luke helped Angie up, Bridget sighed in relief. A ripped sweater was far better than the scattered pieces of a lamp on the tiled floor.

"May I see?" Bridget asked.

Angie looked at Luke, then at Bridget. She held out the torn hem where the stitches had caught on one of Luke's masterpieces and pulled the yarn out.

"Where's your mother?" Bridget asked.

"She goes to the church early to rehearse with the praise team. I usually bring the girls with me," Luke said.

Bridget looked at Angie. Large tears ran down the little girl's face. Inside she felt her chest squeeze. Her mother would have been upset, too, so she took the little girl by the hand. "Come on, I think we can fix this."

Inside the RV, she helped Angie slip out of the ripped sweater and pulled out her broken wooden box.

Lizzy peered in from the doorway.

"So that's what's in there," Lizzy said.

"My granny loved to sew. Mostly embroidery," Bridget said, taking the sweater and inspecting the damage. "She bought this for my mother, and my mother gave it to me. It's one of the last things I have left of her."

She couldn't knit the yarn back together, but she could stitch the gap closed with matching thread. As she worked, Lizzy came in and sat down beside Angie. Luke stayed just inside the doorjamb.

Angie wiped away her tears and sniffled.

When Bridget finished, she saw Luke frown. The stitches were small and neat, just like her mother taught her, but it was apparent the sweater had torn. She looked at the girl's skirts and got an idea.

She rummaged in her box and found a small square of fabric in the same red and black checkered color. She worked the material over the tear and stitched on the patch.

When she was done, Angie grinned. "You fixed it."

Bridget could only hope that Lisa wouldn't mind the fashionable patch on the sweater. Now the girls didn't exactly match as their mother had probably intended.

"Thank you!" Angie surprised her with a hug.

Bridget looked up at Luke, whose white-tooth grin made her feel sappy as a schoolgirl.

Luke and the girls stayed clean for the extra twenty minutes it took Bridget to scramble around the RV and find something suitable to wear. She pulled out a blue cotton dress with white daisies around the bottom edge. Pulling back her hair and twisting it in a bun, she tied it with a piece of ribbon. Tossing clothes everywhere, she located a pair of old ballet flats in yellow.

Pulling a stick of lip gloss out of her purse, she swiped it on her lips.

Outside, Lizzy and Angie sat in the truck. Luke held open the door for her. Tucking a strand of hair behind her ear, feeling self-conscious, she allowed Luke to help her up in the truck. Heat crept in her cheeks as that smile of his made her stomach do a little flip.

Lizzy insisted on sitting next to Bridget in the pews of the church. On the other side of Lizzy, Angie sat swinging her legs and huddled against Luke.

When they rose to sing, Lizzy stood on the pew to see the hymnal book. Kindly, Bridget didn't point out that the little girl couldn't read, but she liked to hold it to the right page. Luke's baritone voice rose above the surrounding others. He had a pleasant voice and seemed to fall into the key much better than she did.

After they sang, the girls headed out into the aisle to join the other children for activities and their lessons in the children's room.

Lisa walked down the aisle, falling short as she spied Bridget beside Luke. Sliding into the aisle, Lisa cleared her throat and pushed past Bridget to get to the other side of Luke. He picked up his hat and put it on his lap to make room for her.

While Luke's sister didn't say a word, the looks between brother and sister made Bridget uncomfortable. She scooted a little away from Luke and prayed the minister wasn't one of those types that made newcomers stand up and introduce themselves. Fortunately, he was not.

Soon, Bridget found it easy to immerse her attention in the pastor's message and forget about Luke's sister on the other

side of him. The message over all too soon brought the children back.

As they filtered out of the church, she heard Lisa ask
Angie, "What is this?"

"Brig-it did it." Lizzy glanced at Bridget and grinned.
Luke explained, but Lisa didn't look any happier. She took the
girls by the hands and headed down the pew.

"You must be Luke's guest out at the farm. I'm so pleased
to meet you." The minister took Bridget's hand as they
headed out the doorway.

"Bridget Wilson, Pastor Lawrence."

"Nice to meet you," Bridget said, trying to pull her hand
back.

"You must forgive me, Luke. I've meant to come out and
visit since I heard the news. How is young James faring? Your
sister said you'd gone to check on the boy."

"Well, considering." Luke placed his hand on Bridget's,
giving it a little tug and keeping it in his custody. Pastor
Lawrence's eyes fell on their intertwined hands. Bridget felt
the eyes of the congregation behind them waiting and watching. She wondered what news this would carry around town
of Luke holding her hand or what Lisa would say about
Angie's cardigan.

"And his mother? How is Sonya?

"Holding up. It will be a few weeks, but they're taken good
care of him in the burn unit."

"Good. Good," said Pastor Lawrence. "I plan on getting
over to the hospital later this week for a visit of my own."

From behind, a man clasped Luke on the shoulder.
"Supper at my place. Barbeque on the new grill."

Pete reached around, offering his hand to Pastor
Lawrence. The other man created a wedge, and Luke moved
her forward. "What can we bring?"

"Oh, just you and your lady friend. Anne's got all the
fixings. You too, Pastor, if you'd like."

"Oh, I wish I could," Pastor Lawrence said.

"See you later." Luke plopped his hat down on his head and escorted Bridget out of the church. They walked to his truck in the rear parking lot. As he held the door open for her, she paused and looked around.

"You okay?" he asked.

"I was looking for the girls." Amazing how she'd grown so attached to them in the time she'd been staying at Luke's farm.

"Lisa takes them to Doug's parents on Sunday afternoons to visit with their grandparents."

She hadn't expected the brief pang of disappointment. She put on a smile as Luke got in the truck. As they pulled out of the parking lot, driving down Main Street, Bridget spied the purple storefront of the salon and thought of Anne. "Did Pete say Anne would be there?"

"I'd hope. Anne is his wife." Luke chuckled.

"As in Anne from the hair salon?" Bridget could hope. It was a small town. How many Annes could there be?

"She was at the diner when I picked you up."

Bridget sat deeper in her seat. "I like Anne."

"Anne's a good friend," Luke said, keeping his eyes on the road. Looking out the window, Bridget noticed they weren't headed for the farm. Luke turned off Main Street in the opposite direction.

He glanced over at her. "I hope you don't mind. I usually go out to the home and have lunch with my mom on Sundays. She'll be expecting me."

Bridget didn't know how to feel about this. She'd heard Pete's remark about bringing home a girl, and even though he hadn't said it, he'd made her feel like a piece of trash. Would Luke's mom feel the same? It wasn't as if she and Luke were … together.

Bridget smoothed down the wrinkles in the front of her dress. "Are you sure you want to take me?"

Luke reached over, his warm hand covering her fidgeting one. "I understand if it is uncomfortable for you. My mom doesn't remember things well anymore. Sometimes she doesn't remember Lisa or me at all."

"I'm sorry, Luke. That must be very hard for you all." Bridget squeezed his hand.

"They serve ham dinners on Sundays at home. The pies come from the Main Street Diner. Gwen makes the best apple pie in three counties."

Like a man, he is always thinking of food. Bridget shook her head. "If that's your way of trying to convince me to go with you to visit your mother, I suppose I'll have to admit you sold me on the pie." Even though she didn't know exactly how she felt about visiting with his mother, it seemed she and Luke had gotten close suddenly. Maybe a bit too sudden, as she didn't plan on staying here or getting involved with anyone. Especially if it meant trusting someone again.

A little while later, Bridget and Luke walked down the red-carpeted hall at Woodcrest Manor to his mother's room. Dark walls and the silence made her wonder if they weren't at a funeral home. Grateful, she never had enough money to put her grandmother in a nursing home. She'd had all the needed care provided right at home. As cozy as they made it feel, this place reminded her more of a hospital for dying than it did a home for retired and elderly needing assistance.

Her heart went out to Luke as they headed down another hallway. Three doors down, he took off his hat and stepped inside a room with a bed and a chair facing the windows looking out at the gardens beyond. Bridget would have never guessed the pepper-haired lady sitting in the chair with an afghan on her lap could be Luke's mother.

"Ready for our lunch date, Momma?"

Bridget stayed by the door as the woman glanced up from her puzzle. "There you are. I was beginning to wonder if you forgot about me."

Bridget could see the relief on Luke's face. He bent down on one knee and kissed the older woman's cheek. "And here I was, worried you wouldn't know who I was."

Even in his jest, Bridget recognized the sorrow in his voice.

"Mommas, don't ever forget." She wagged her hand at him. Bridget shifted, and the other woman turned her head. "Are you my daughter? Lisa?"

Luke rose to his feet. He held out his hand for Bridget to come closer. "Mom, this is my friend, Bridget Wilson. Bridget, my mother, Darla Myers."

Darla's gaze swept over Bridget, then returned to Luke. "You brought her here before?"

Luke shook his head. "No, Mom, you're thinking of Lisa. I haven't brought anyone here to visit with you before."

Bridget put her hand on his arm. His muscles tensed under her touch. "It is nice to meet you, Mrs. Myers. I'm looking forward to our lunch together."

Luke put his hand by his mouth. "Don't let her fool you, Mom. She's only here for the pie."

Bridget slapped his arm, and he jumped. It made Darla laugh.

They had lunch in the dining hall of the home. Luke carried his mother's food tray, and Bridget helped ensure Mrs. Myers had a good window seat.

"Would you like to take a walk after lunch?" Luke asked his mother.

Darla waved him off. "My legs can't carry me as far as they used to, but I'm good with looking." She sighed.

"I'm sure they have a wheelchair. Luke's a strong guy. He can push you. The gardens are probably lovelier outside than through the window." Bridget glanced at Luke.

"Not allowed outside," Darla muttered. "Got a room with a view."

Luke grimaced. "Lisa isn't here, Mom. You want to go out to the gardens. I'll take you out in the gardens."

Darla's gaze dropped to her tray of food. "I'd like that. I'd like it very much."

By the time they finished lunch, Luke had found a nurse willing to get them a wheelchair. They took Darla out to the small garden between the two nursing home buildings. She sat quietly as Luke pushed her.

Bridget waited for the questions to come. Where are you from? What do you do? How did you meet? They never came. Instead, Darla pointed out flowers. She seemed to like the yellow roses the best and remarked on Bridget's yellow shoes.

Soon though, Darla's mind strayed as Luke warned, "It's time we go back."

Darla didn't object, and as Bridget helped Luke tuck the afghan over his mother's legs, Darla said, "I like this one. Maybe you could come back sometime."

"Every Sunday," Luke promised. He kissed his mother's cheek and settled his hat back on his head. Darla put her hand over it, blushing like a schoolgirl.

"You'd better watch yourself, young man. I'm a married woman."

"Yes, ma'am."

Outside the nursing home, Luke walked Bridget to his old truck.

"Every Sunday?" she asked.

"I can't take care of her. I wish I could. Lisa's got work and the girls. After my dad died, her mind started slipping. Little things, then one day she drove over to the next town and forgot where home was, that kind of thing."

Bridget stepped close to him and wrapped her arms around him. She could hear his rattled breath. A moment later, his arms wrapped around her. "You're a good son. A good man. I can see why you have so many friends in this town."

She rested her cheek against his shoulder, absorbing the smells of grease and long grasses. Everything about this man-made her heartache. Did he know how much the people in this town probably loved him? How much she loved him?

Her heart hammered in her chest. Luke pulled her closer, his hand sliding down the side of her face. There was no way he could have felt that, could he?

She stared into his eyes, lost for words. His face tilted, bending toward her. Bridget gulped. Rising on her tiptoes, her forehead rammed into the bill of his hat, and she jerked away. Luke twisted out of her arms, bending to retrieve his hat. Bridget hopped into the truck, her cheeks hot and embarrassed, and avoided looking at him.

"I guess we should get back. I have a few things that need tending before we head to Pete's later."

Bridget could only nod in agreement.

9

"Mrs. Shaw will bring the girls home around eight this evening. They'll be washed so they'll need their jammies before bed," Lisa informed Luke as he came around the house from his basement apartment.

"Then I suspect you should be here when they arrive." He had a lawn chair in each hand.

"Where are you going?" Lisa stepped in front of him. "It's Sunday. You know I have my meeting with the ladies tonight about the festival."

"Pete's." Luke held up the lawn chairs. "It's Sunday."

Lisa didn't budge. Luke sidestepped and went around her. "I suppose you're taking that woman with you? Did you see what she did to Angie's sweater?"

Luke put both lawn chairs in one hand. "I thought she did a good job patching it up and covering the rip."

Lisa's eyes narrowed. "It would have been nice if she hadn't ripped it to begin with."

"What do you expect with the girls running around the shed in their Sunday best? They're kids. They get dirty. Lucky, Bridget had a needle and thread and knew how to use it."

"Well, maybe you shouldn't have them out before church." Lisa crossed her arms.

"It's never been a problem before. And if you don't like it, take them to church with you when you go." Luke could practically see her calculating her revenge like when they were kids to get her way. Lord, help him. He didn't have the tolerance for it at this moment like he should. He shouldn't have said it, and there was no taking it back, either. Not that it didn't need to be said. In the years since Lisa returned home without Doug, his older sister turned more bitter by the day.

He loved those girls, but sometimes, a man needed to go places without babysitting all the time. Lisa kept pushing those girls on him and the Shaws as if they'd become more of a bother than a blessing. He'd needed to call her out on it for a while now.

He didn't want to see Lizzy and Angie suffer, nor did he want to have them along for his date with Bridget. Stunned by his own admission, he stared blankly at Lisa.

"Fine. And I'll just tell Mrs. Shaw she can take the girls to Pete's, and you'll bring them home."

Luke put down the lawn chairs. "Your meeting better be over by eight, so you can meet the Shaws here. I don't mind watching the girls all week while you work, but I am headed over to Pete's for the barbecue."

"You're taking *her*, aren't you?"

It was more of a question than a statement, so he didn't answer her.

"You want her to stay here? You like her? Please tell me you didn't take her to see Mom." Lisa's jaw dropped. "What were you thinking?"

Luke could only stand there, pretending to listen as Lisa carried on even as he went over and over in his mind his feelings. He'd let them get in the way of his commitments to his family, to his sister. He'd acted selfishly. His attraction to

Bridget had distracted him from concentrating on those he loved.

Luke gritted his teeth and tried not to allow Lisa to rattle him too much. Finding a pause for Lisa to take a breath, Luke hiked up the lawn chairs. "Sometimes, it is nice to have others you can depend on. Not all of us still have our family to rely on."

He gave her one last chance to protest.

She opened her mouth and inhaled.

He held his breath.

Lisa made a strangled sound in her voice and stomped off towards the house. He made a note to take it up with God later in prayer.

∽

Pete and his wife, Anne, lived in the newer part of town.

The massive grill Luke made sat on the back patio, and they invited Luke to fire it up before the rest of the guests arrived. Bridget spotted Anne, who waved, talking with a group of ladies.

Several children raced through the backyard and rounded the tables and chairs, but Bridget kept her distance, feeling suddenly out of place.

Yet, Anne waved and motioned for Bridget to join them. Anne introduced her to Megan, Dorothy, and Anne's mother, Barbara. The older ladies smiled politely at her, and Anne explained she worked with Luke. It didn't stop the questions. "Have you been working for Luke long?" And "Where you staying dear?"

"Why don't you help me get the table set?" Anne suggested, and Bridget readily agreed. Anne laid her hand on Bridget's arm, "Don't mind them. They're curious and mean well."

They set out the paper plates and plastic utensils while the men gathered around the grill. It didn't take long for others to arrive and fill the backyard.

"It's just like Luke to give Pete that big ole mammoth of a grill," said Dorothy fanning herself with a paper plate. Her pale yellow blouse was a shade lighter than her capris pants. She grinned as Megan, the oldest of the trio of women, came to join them.

"Well, I can tell you, seeing the way my Bert is up there, drooling all over it, that he's praying that Luke will make another one," Megan said.

"Seems a shame a man like that would waste all that talent on a heap of junk." Anne's mother, Barbara, clucked her tongue. Anne's mother didn't look a day other than forty. Her hairstyle curled and fluffed, giving away her age more than the crow's feet by her eyes. Her grandmother would have told her some people couldn't move on from the time, and rightly so.

She wasn't sure why, but Bridget disliked Anne's mother. She'd just met the woman, but the remark about Luke didn't sit well with her. Luke came home when his family needed him. He didn't need talent to do what was right. His heart was in the right place, and she pulled back her shoulders about to say so when Bridget said, "I'm sure Luke would be more than happy to make another one."

Barbara snorted. "Not unless Luke salvages another perfectly good stove from somewhere. I wouldn't think any of those up there should get their hopes up."

All the ladies turned their attention onto the deck, where the men stood around the grill like a newborn baby.

"If I know my Bert, he's up there trying to convince Luke to make him one just like it. Probably even offering to pay for it, too." Megan shook her head and looked back at the rest of the ladies.

"I'd watch your stove if I were you," Anne warned, "You might just be finding yours out on the street next Tuesday."

Megan's eyes grew large, then she laughed. "Wouldn't that just be something Bert would do? Get me a new stove so he could get Luke to make him a grill?"

Bridget tilted her head and studied Luke up on the deck. He leaned against the railing, sipping a soda and waving a hand as he spoke. Modest. He wouldn't brag or boast about the grill. Not the Luke she'd come to know these past few days.

"I wonder if he'd charge you to pick it up or just take it for free?" Dorothy said.

Anne leaned over near Bridget. "Luke picks up the trash on Tuesday mornings for the town, but you probably already knew that."

Why didn't that surprise her? A man had to make a living, somehow, right? But he'd been a professional ballplayer, and now ... he collected junk and picked up trash for the town. On top of it, he took care of his family and the animals on the farm, and she knew the horses belonged to Lisa, thanks to little Lizzy's endless supply of information.

She had a whole new respect for a guy who'd give up fame and fortune to take care of his family. Bridget could appreciate what Luke had done.

"Luke doesn't seem the kind of guy who'd do it unless he wanted to do it."

If any of the ladies heard, they paid her comment no mind, but Anne did. Bridget could see it in her eyes.

She liked Anne. She was the first person in the town to welcome her into this new place. She planned on staying for a short time. Not that things were different, with Luke offering her commission to sell his junk. However, thinking of leaving and not seeing Luke anymore made her insides twist uncomfortably.

The women continued to chat around her. All the pleasantries of introduction had faded as Anne took the liberty to introduce everyone to her.

"Oh, I might have a job for you," Anne said, moving away from the group. Bridget followed Anne to a table set up at the end of the deck and poured them a glass of iced tea. "Mother is going away next week with a few ladies in the church on a retreat. I hoped maybe you could be of help for the weekend."

Bridget took the drink and sipped, trying to hide her smile. "It's only a few days, right? I am sure Luke wouldn't mind. He kind of gave me a job. More like an arrangement, but I'm going to sell his stuff for him."

Anne choked over her iced tea. Bridget patted her back, and like she was a child putting, Anne's hands went straight up.

"My goodness, Anne," Barbara said.

"You okay?" Megan asked.

Anne took a deep breath and let her hands drop to her sides. If Bridget would have known that the information about her new arrangement with Luke would cause such a commotion, she wouldn't have said anything.

"I'm fine. Just fine." Anne gulped.

"I just told her about Luke opening a shop, and he's gonna start selling his stuff."

Silence stretched between the ladies. Each one of them looked at the other. Megan raised her slim brows, and Barbara's mouth worked, but no words escaped.

Bridget didn't think that happened very much to the older lady.

Shame on her. Didn't this morning's message teach us to be kind to one's neighbor and love one another?

She'd sat soaking in each word of Pastor Lawrence's message, like a thirsty person in the desert who couldn't find a quench to the ache they had inside. Sitting there beside Luke, sharing his Bible, and listening to the beautiful songs of the praise team had stirred a longing in her she'd left behind long ago.

Now with these women, she didn't know where she

belonged. They seemed so familiar, like old friends, when she walked over at Anne's invitation. Yet, they were strangers.

Lisa came around the corner of the house. Lizzy and Angie ran out from around her toward a large oak tree where the other kids played. A few girls sat with dolls on a blanket while the other children chased each other in a game of tag.

Bridget's spine stiffened.

"Luke told me how you fixed Angie's sweater. My mother made those sweaters for the girls a few months ago. The first time they'd worn them. Anyway, I just wanted to say thank you," Lisa said.

"It was my pleasure," Bridget said.

Bridget looked over at the girls. Tension, thick and muggy, grew between them as Lisa approached. Bridget fiddled with the ties of her blouse.

"Seems with Mrs. Wagner's death and Katie Carter not feeling well, our festival meeting had to be postponed. I hope you don't mind the girls and I dropping in, Anne. Luke said you and Pete were having folks over tonight."

Anne glanced at Bridget and then her mother. "Of course, you are always welcome."

Barbara narrowed her eyes. "Don't you usually visit your momma on Sundays? I'm sure she'd be disappointed not to see you today."

"Luke and I had lunch with her today. She is such a sweet woman," Bridget said.

Lisa looked at her, and a chill sent prickles down Bridget's arms. More so from disappointment, for a moment, she'd almost believed that Lisa had come to make peace. Why should she think now that the woman had changed her mind about her after a few stitches of a sweater?

"That was very nice, I'm sure Darla appreciated it." Barbara turned as two boys started shouting, and fists were raised.

"Pete!" Anne called, pointing to the boys. "There they go again!"

"Boys!" Pete took off in a long stride across the yard.

"Oh, those boys. When they get into arguments like that, they're their father's dealing with." Anne placed her hands on her hips.

"Oh, that reminds me, how is Doug? Have you heard from him?"

Barbara asked Lisa.

"No." Lisa tilted up her chin and stepped away. "I'll just go check on the girls."

A hint of amusement crossed Barbara's face, and Anne touched Bridget's arm. "Don't pay her any mind. That girl has got issues she's got to work on."

All the other ladies nodded in agreement.

"I think I see some burgers hitting plates. Should we grab the cold stuff from the fridge?" Megan asked.

By cold stuff, the ladies brought a tossed salad Megan made, Dorothy's potato salad, and fruit salad.

"We were to bring something?" Bridget asked, panicked. She came empty-handed.

"Luke's contribution of the grill has you both covered," Anne laughed

"For a while, I'd say." Megan pointed again to the men making noises and drooling over the grill. They all had a good laugh.

A few more people came, stepping off the deck and into the backyard. Luke gave her a tug on the arm and led her through the food line.

Burgers sautéed with onions and mushrooms smelled divine, and she poured steak sauce over the top of the cheese without a bun. She'd never smelled burgers so good.

Luke smashed two burgers on his plate and filled the space with potato salad. They sat at the end of a table, but no one seemed to sit near them.

Lisa stood beside Dorothy and a few other couples Bridget saw arrive but couldn't remember their names. Occasionally, Lisa would glance over her shoulder, give Bridget a sly smile, and return to her conversation.

When they finished eating, Luke opened lawn chairs in the yard for them. Several of the older folks sat, and some other adults joined in with the kids for a ball game. Luke stood in the center as the pitcher.

"I haven't seen a lawn chair like that before," a woman near Lisa walking past her remarked. "Is that one of your brother's inventions?"

Bridget tried not to laugh. She kept an eye watching Luke's play. She had scooted her lawn chair near Anne's when the woman approached. "I made it. Well, I braided new twine through it since the ribbons were busted."

"How clever. Are you going to sit in it?" the woman asked.

"I wouldn't risk it if I were you, Brenda," Lisa said, standing beside the woman.

"Are you insinuating I'm too heavy?" Brenda glowered at Lisa.

"Never." Lisa tugged down her tee shirt. "I just didn't want you getting hurt, is all."

"It's perfectly safe. You're welcome to use it." Bridget stepped out of the way for her to sit in the chair.

Anne came from grabbing a refill of soda on the deck. "Did you make that?"

Bridget nodded, feeling a bit of pride but too embarrassed with Lisa staring at her.

"You should make more of these. You could sell them at the festival, couldn't she, Lisa?"

"Oh yeah," said Betty. "I'd buy one for sitting and watching the parade down the street."

"Well, I don't know about that," Lisa said.

"You're still taking applications for vendors, aren't you? The festival's still a couple of weeks away. Bridget would have plenty of time to make some. I'm sure Luke can get her the parts, and who knows what else he has in that shed to sell."

"I like that idea." Bridget's mind spun with possibilities, the saleswoman in her kicking in.

Lisa crossed her arms. "Luke has already got a lot going on with helping with the festival. I'd hate to see my brother stuck with one more thing on his list. Besides, I'm sure Bridget is planning on leaving well before the festival."

"You are?" asked Anne.

"She's right. I can't live in the RV forever, but I think I can stick around for the festival. It sounds fun."

Behind them, shouts and cheers echoed through the back-yard. She glanced over her shoulder, watching Luke chase a young boy to first base. He could have reached the boy but made it look like he tried hard as the boy hit his foot into the bag.

When she glanced back, Lisa, Brenda, Anne, and Megan had taken all the seats behind her. With their heads bent together, they spoke of the festival to come. Feeling out of place, Bridget headed to the tree where Angie sat with two other girls dressing dolls. Lizzy bounced in the furthest part of the yard, part of the outfield in the game.

She sat beside the girls and asked, "Got room for one more?"

Angie said little, and she handed Bridget a doll. "This one is Samantha. You can pretend you're her."

Bridget ran her hand down over the doll's hair. She glanced over at Lisa and the group of women, then at Luke playing baseball with the boys.

"You're supposed to get dressed for the dance at the festi-val," Angie nudged her.

"Sorry," Bridget said.

"You want to look nice for Uncle Luke at the festival, don't you?" Angie's soft and sweet voice sent a flutter in h

10

Late Monday afternoon, Lizzy and Angie dressed in their oldest play clothes. Lizzy dragged a bucket she'd found in the shop, and Luke filled it with warm soapy water. They helped Bridget wash the grime from some of the junk masterpieces Luke had created over the years.

Inside, Luke tinkered with another gas stove. He had enough parts to construct another version of the grill he'd given Pete. Not an exact replica, but close enough. Too soon, he heard the squeals and laughter, and as he poked his head out, he found the girls having a soap suds fight. Bridget sat soaked with an empty bucket near the windows.

Luke bent over to pick up a discarded rag. At the same time, Bridget picked up her bucket, and as Luke straightened, she tossed the contents. The soapy water splashed against his chest, and the girls ran into the parking lot.

Bridget dropped the bucket. Her hands covered her mouth. Angie and Lizzy giggled and danced around him.

"I'm so sorry. I didn't mean ..." Bridget couldn't stop laughing.

Luke bit his lip. His shirt stuck to him, and water-soaked his jeans.

Angie and Lizzy both crept up beside him, covering their mouths too. But giggles still escaped.

Luke tried to make his sternest face at the girls. Yet his eyes wouldn't leave Bridget. Her eyes widened to the size of his mother's teacup saucers. Beneath her hands, he heard her snicker with laughter.

"You think this is funny?" he asked.

Angie and Lizzy stepped away from him. Their giggles ceased. Both girls stared between him and Bridget.

She shook her head. Bridget laughed, snorted, then laughed again.

"You know I'm all wet, right?" He took a step towards her.

Bridget nodded.

"Uncle Luke …. Uncle Luke …" Lizzy ran up and tugged on his shirt.

Luke looked down at his niece.

"She didn't mean it. She didn't," Lizzy said.

Luke cringed at the stricken look on Lizzy and Angie's faces. He couldn't help it. A man had to do what a man had to do, and that was precisely what he intended.

He picked up a nearby bucket, still half full of dirty, sudsy water.

"You wouldn't …" Bridget stopped laughing.

She held her hands out in front of her and took a step back.

Luke took a step forward. He knew he grinned for the sheer pleasure of what he was about to do.

Lizzy and Angie both grabbed hold of one of his legs.

"Hey, whose side are you on?" he asked.

"Don't do it, Uncle Luke." Lizzy squeezed his leg tighter.

"It was an accident," Angie said.

Bridget took another step back. "They're right, you know. Listen to them."

"Traitors," Luke growled.

Bridget's gaze darted around her for escape.

He raised the bucket, and Bridget rushed toward him. As Luke swung the bucket back, ready to propel, Bridget grabbed it and pushed it down. Together, they drenched both little girls.

Angie and Lizzy squealed and dashed away as the water sloshed over their heads.

Now, Luke decided it was his turn to laugh.

Bridget leaned against him, laying her head on his shoulder, and laughed. For a second, he forgot the merriment and wrapped his arm around her, pulling her close. She smelled like liquid soap; nothing beyond heaven could have smelt better.

As his gaze met hers, they both stopped laughing. Behind him, the sounds of giggling girls became mute. His gaze fell on her soft pink lips.

Sliding his hand against the side of her face, drawing her closer. The radiance of the sunlight danced across the damp tendrils of her dark hair to frame her sweet face. Her tongue darted out to lick her lips. Luke tilted his head and leaned closer. She wanted to kiss him, too. She wasn't trying very hard to stop him or step away.

Bridget's hand came up against his chest. His heart thundered underneath her palm as he waited to see if she'd push him away. Instead, the sound of two little girls interjected.

"Luke and Brig-It up in a tree. K. I. S. S. I. N. G." Lizzy's voice rang out. She danced around them in a wide circle. Skipping and singing.

"Gross." Angie made a face.

Luke and Bridget both started laughing.

"I'm going to tell Momma," Angie said.

Then as if a cold shower had been poured down over the top of her, Bridget shivered and pulled away.

"You'll do nothing of the sort," Luke said.

The way Lisa liked to gossip, Pastor Lawrence would be here by the morning, giving him a lecture on the sanctity of marriage. He shouldn't have pulled Bridget in his arms like that in front of the girls, but he'd been caught up in the moment. Lifting his cap and running his hand through his hair, he took a deep breath. He couldn't believe he almost kissed her in front of the girls. Forget Pastor Lawrence. Lisa would have his head.

Glancing at Bridget, he watched her bend down, collecting the empty buckets.

"Here, let me help with that," he said.

"No, that's okay. I think you've all done enough for one day."

The side of her neck was an adorable shade of pink. He reached over to push a piece of wet hair from her neck when she jerked away. Her eyes went to the girls. She shoved the buckets at him. "I need to go dry off."

Lizzy came up beside Luke and tugged on his shirt. "Uncle Luke, you gonna marry Brig-It?"

"Why do you say that?" Luke asked.

"Cause you kissed her. People kiss when they get married," Lizzy said.

"I didn't kiss her." Luke handed each of the girls a bucket.

"Did too." Lizzy crossed her arms, not wanting the bucket.

"Their lips didn't touch." Angie rolled her eyes and took both buckets. "Come on. We got to clean up before Momma sees us."

Lizzy pouted. "I wanted to see you kiss Brig-It. Then you two can get married. I like Brig-It."

"I like her, too, pumpkin." Luke led the girls over to the house, got them dry, and gave them a snack. As they ate, he watched out the window for the woman who made his heart hit a grand slam inside. Lord, help him. He was falling in love with Bridget.

～

On Wednesday, Luke waited for Bridget outside the barn. He knew she'd be headed into town to give Anne a hand in the salon and wanted to catch her. She'd slipped out at dawn the day before, and he didn't enjoy thinking she'd avoided him.

"Headed to town?" he asked.

"Anne asked me to help in the salon again. Is there something you need?" she asked.

He took her by surprise. She'd slicked her hair back into a ponytail and put on another one of those cute little skirts he saw her in often.

"I thought I'd give you a ride. I've got some business in town this morning, and I can pick you up later."

She glanced in the house's direction. "What about the girls?"

"Lisa's not going to work until this afternoon." He shoved his hands in his pockets and rocked on his heels.

"There's no need. I can ride my bike. That way, I'll have it to come back." Hitching the strap of her satchel over her shoulder, she walked past him.

"The church has a baseball tournament during the festival, a town thing. The kids have practice late this afternoon. With Sonya in Louisville with Jimmy, I hoped you might want to be my right hand. You know, since we're partners and all."

"Partners?" she asked.

"Well, we're working together, so we're partners."

She tilted her head and gave him a look. Her eyes narrowed a bit. He couldn't hold back his smile. He held out his hand and offered it to her, then realized his mistake. She looked at his hand. She seemed to consider his request. Tugging down on her blouse and straightening that cute little skirt she had on. Yellow, she looked good in that color.

Then again, he'd probably like her in any color. He tipped up his hat and rubbed his head. She would not make this easy on him. He could see in her eyes. The uncertainty.

As she reached for it, he laid his hand on her arm. "I just

thought maybe you could step in and give a hand. I mean, if you don't want to, I get it."

"I planned on doing a few things in town after helping Anne. But I suppose I could do them another time."

"Anything I can help with?"

Her cheeks turned a little pink. "There's a matter of banking … You know, for the website."

"I can take you by the bank this morning if you have time. Lisa works there, but we can get you hooked up with an account of your own, and that way, you can just pay me from the website."

She pulled back her shoulders. "You don't have to do that."

"It's business. We're partners, remember."

Her pink her cheeks got a little pinker. "Not everyone around here might think that. You know I'm not staying, right?"

Luke had seen Bridget sitting with Angie at the picnic and playing with dolls while Lisa and the other women visited. Knowing Lisa, they'd spoken of town and festivals and things Bridget wouldn't feel included in. He understood feeling misplaced. After leaving Hidden Hills for the big leagues and coming home, he didn't see things the same way anymore.

But he'd lived here almost all his life. He knew these people, and Bridget didn't, except maybe Anne. He said a silent prayer of thanks for friendship to Bridget, hoping they would become good friends. After all, God knew more than he did. Bridget needed the blessing of good friends.

He added a little side note to his prayer, hoping God would help Bridget find that in Hidden Hills. Hoping she'd one day feel comfortable calling this place home.

He hadn't thought about it until now; he wanted her to stay. He hoped he hadn't screwed it up by kissing her, but he'd do it again.

"So how bout you help me, and this afternoon, I'll show you how we play ball here in Hidden Hills."

"Are you sure you want me to help you?" She adjusted the strap of her purse on her shoulder.

"Would I ask if I wasn't?"

She seemed to consider what he said. And then a faint smile crossed her lips. "Well … if you're sure. I'd be happy to."

On the drive to town, his hand itched to take hold of hers, but he gripped the steering wheel and held it there instead, focusing on getting her to town. He'd never been good around girls. Even as a teenager, he had been awkward, and as a grown man, he'd been the shy and silent type. As the first baseman for the Louisville Sluggers, there had been girls: flirtatious girls, fangirls, crazy girls. And while they hung on him and hugged him as he went past, they were just fans, and he kept on moving. None of them had struck his heart. Or made him think twice about wanting a family or being with somebody like thinking about Bridget did.

He pulled up in front of Anne's hair salon. He reached across Bridget and pushed open the door. His face close to hers, he gave her a quick peck on the cheek. She didn't pull away. She scooted quickly out of the truck. "I'll see you later."

11

Oh Lord, Bridget thought, *how did I ever get myself in a mess like this one?* Luke was turning out to be more than just a knight in shining armor. If she didn't find a way to get out of this little town, she feared she'd never leave because of her heart.

At first, she told herself it was the town and the friendly people living there. But she knew better. The moment Luke kissed her, he'd branded her heart.

She couldn't afford to love a man like Luke.

She simply didn't feel worthy. How could she bring her debts onto a man so kind, compassionate, so ... She rested her chin in her hands as she watched him from a set of steel bleachers.

Upon arrival, Luke knew each kid by name, and Bridget sat on the clipboard beside her. There were no tryouts for this team. Luke explained to her every kid got his turn to play. There were seventeen of them in all — boys and girls. Each player wore a dark blue T-shirt with a bank logo on the front and a number on the back.

He tossed a ball from the pitcher's mound of the town's Little League baseball field. One at a time, the kids took a turn at bat, rotating positions around the baseball field. Luke insisted Bridget come and help him with the roster.

Angie came up to bat. Luke took a few steps toward the home plate. Angie tipped up her red helmet and swung her wooden bat.

"Ready? Keep your eye on the ball," Luke said.

Tired of throwing the ball in the air and trying to catch it, Lizzy scooted up the bleachers beside Bridget.

"I thought you were out there playing." Bridget glanced over at Lizzy. Her hair was in two little ponytails, and her feet swung back and forth.

"Are you crazy?" Lizzy said. "They throw balls at you if you play out there!"

Bridget couldn't suppress her laugh. "I heard they do that in baseball."

Lizzy shrugged and watched as Angie took a swing and missed. Bridget called out, "You can do it, Angie!"

Several other parents sat on the bleachers, some reading a book or fidgeting with their phones. Lisa had dropped off the girls and left for work. She wondered how much time these two little girls spent with their momma.

Angie looked over and smiled at Bridget's cry of encouragement. Luke spoke to her, keeping her focused on him, on the ball. When Angie swung this time, the bat hit the ball. "Go. Go. Go!" Luke said.

Bridget jumped up and down and clapped as Angie tagged first base. With the ball returned to his glove, Luke glanced and winked at her.

Bridget's cheeks grew a little hot.

"Are you going to marry Uncle Luke?" Lizzy asked.

A dozen little butterflies took off inside Bridget's stomach. Trying hard to hide it, she tilted her head and looked at the little girl. "Now, why would I do that?"

Not that the idea hadn't come across her mind a time or two.

"Momma says that Uncle Luke was going to marry Jimmy's mom until you came along." Lizzy crossed her ankles and swung her legs back and forth again.

"Oh, she did, did she?"

Lizzy nodded. "Yep, Momma says that's why she sent him to see Jimmy, but he came home with you instead."

She watched as a boy took a swing at the ball Luke threw.

"Strike one," the catcher, not more than ten years old, called from behind a catcher's mask.

"I have no intention of marrying your uncle." Another reason she needed to return to the city. Her hand went to her cheek. She needed to stop thinking of Luke as more than a friend. *Not that he would have her. Or that he'd even asked.*

"Did you come from a trash can?" Lizzy asked.

The boy swung again, "Strike two!"

Bridget sighed. "You're too smart for your own good. You know that?"

Lizzy grinned. "Momma says I'm the most 'pertinent girl at church."

"I think you mean prettiest," Bridget said.

"No. Momma says …"

"I think I've heard enough of what your momma has to say for today. Why don't we see what we can do to help your uncle?" Bridget's voice crackled with irritation. It wasn't Lizzy's fault that her mother liked to gossip, nor was she right.

Was that how the people of this town saw her? Is that why Anne let her go early today? Because her customers weren't showing up with Bridget there?

Going back to the city would be the best thing. And for her and Luke's sake, it was best if she just forgot about that kiss and moved on. The sooner, the better.

∼

On Wednesday, Anne didn't need her help. Bridget parked her bicycle and walked down the sidewalk, glancing into the empty windows of a building. Across from her, a gas station and a bit of land with a gazebo beckoned her forward. Further down the street, she could smell the coffee and grease from the local diner where she and Anne often had lunch or coffee. She spotted a library no bigger than one of the little houses she first passed on her walk. She'd probably walked past it a dozen times and hadn't noticed until today.

She found it quaint with white siding and large, bright, glass windows. Signs and posters to encourage passers-by to read greeted her. In a small town like this, they would have to advertise. Else people wouldn't notice.

Not that there was much else in this place. She frowned, opening the door, then relaxed when no bell sounded above. Inside, she found a parlor filled with books, a table with chairs, and a counter with two elderly ladies sitting behind it. "Well, hello there, dear."

"Can we help you?" asked the other.

Bridget shook her head and smiled. She breathed in deeply. This place smelled like books and polished wood... and a hint of dust hiding between the shelves. "I don't think so. I can find a spot and browse a few books if you don't have a problem with that?"

As if the two women had never heard of spending time in a library, the taller and younger of the two said, "Are you looking for something?"

With little to do in her RV and all of Luke's junk around her, she figured catching up on her reading couldn't hurt. Maybe find a few craft books to make some things since she'd filled out the application and used some of her money from helping Anne to pay the fee for the festival. Luke had a bunch of large pieces to sell, but some smaller stuff would bring more sales and draw people. At least, she figured from experience, it could hurt none to try. She brushed her hand over a row of books.

"I've not seen you around here before." The shorter woman slid her reading glasses down her nose. She held a card in her hand, freshly stamped, and slid it into the back pocketed sleeve inside the back cover of a book.

Clearly, technology and bar-coded books with scanners hadn't reached the priority list for running this library. Simplistically, Bridget liked this place. For however long she remained here, she enjoyed knowing some places in the world could thrive and be content with themselves as they always had been. But, a pang for Lexington, Shelby, and public transportation shifted to an ache, a reminder of what put her there in the first place.

"I'm not from around here." She didn't know why she felt the need to explain. "I'm just visiting for a little while." How long, she didn't know.

"You'll need a library card if you're to take any books out of here with you."

"And don't forget to return them." The shorter one pointed a finger at her.

"Oh, I don't think I'll take any along with me today. I'm not sure what I'm looking for." More truth than she realized.

"What's your name?" A smile straightened the wrinkles of the taller woman's lips.

"Bridget."

"It's nice to meet you, Bridget. I'm Marge, and this here is my sister Maeve. Were you looking for a romance novel or two?" Marge wiggled her brows.

"We don't keep the steamy sort here. You'll have to go to the county library if you're looking for *that*." Maeve's stare bored into her as if the older woman tried to see inside her soul.

Good luck with that.

"No. No. Not that." Bridget didn't know if coming here was a good idea. "You don't have any magazines like HGTV or books on upholstery or DIY, do you?"

Marge tilted her head to the side, tapping a finger against her lip in thought.

"Sounds like you're confused and came in the wrong building. If you're fixin' something, you'll want the Top Shop on the street below, or there's the hardware over in Shelbyville. Luke Myers might have something in his junk piles for what you're looking for."

"Maeve. She came looking for a book." Marge scowled at her sister.

"Luke's bound to have a fix-it manual or two." Maeve shrugged.

"I've been to Luke's place, and that's why I'd like to find a book or two on how to fix things up. Maybe get an idea for some other things he has lying about his place." She tried not to pinch the bridge of her nose, which she did when flustered and annoyed.

"She's been to Luke's." Maeve gave Marge a look of matter-of-fact.

"You're a friend of Lisa's?"

Maeve leaned close to the counter.

"No. Not really." She hoped they wouldn't press her anymore. Slightly surprised, they hadn't already heard or knew who she was. Didn't gossip spread fast in a small town?

Marlene turned away. She walked around the counter, went up a stair to a new landing, and pulled out a drawer, flicking through the card catalog cards.

"Here it is!" Marge held up the card. "We've had a few of them. Come, let me show you."

"Out the door," she heard Maeve mutter behind her as she followed Marge up the stairs and into the far corner of another room. Marge fished out the books and held them out to her. "Will any of these do?"

Bridget took the books, one thicker than her old college textbooks, and written several decades before she was born. The other thin, with instructions for pillows and painting techniques for furniture. As she flipped through the pages, Marlene pointed to the bottom shelf. "There are a few more down there. I'd grab them for you, but my joints don't bend like they used to anymore."

"Thank you. I'll look through them. Is there a place I can sit?"

"In the front by the window. There is a table with chairs." A set of crow's feet spread from the corners of the older woman's eyes, but the light in them, the kindness, still showed through and warmed Bridget in a way she hadn't felt since her grandmother passed away.

Marlene left her there in the corner. After a while, Bridget lowered herself to the floor. First, to see the books down there, then to read, as it was as good as spot as any. Before she knew it, she sat Indian-style with her legs crossed and a pile of books on her lap and her mind filled with ideas.

She would surprise him, she decided, leaving him with a few items in his junk pile refurbished to sell for the trouble she caused him by bringing her here. However long it may be. Sitting on the floor had made her legs grow stiff, and an ache formed in her tailbone, causing her to rise to elevate it.

She'd laid two books aside, debated on a third, and noted its title for when she came back again. If she came back again, she hadn't intended to go inside the library, nor had she planned to borrow any of the books, but the idea had been spur-of-the-moment, as had fixing up a thing or two for Luke.

He'd fixed the shower in the RV for her. He'd even turned on a propane tank, so she had warm water instead of cold for washing.

It made her smile. For a man who picked her up, like he did the other pieces of junk he brought home, he had care about him. Then she caught herself, shook her head, and reminded herself she couldn't stay. She couldn't keep letting her heart attach to him. Falling in love with Luke Myers would only bring more trouble.

Except she already had.

12

With the festival a few days away, Luke spent his time between baseball practice with the kids and helping at the church. He, Pete, and Sam Brink worked on setting up the church's outdoor kitchen tent, where they planned to sell all kinds of baked goods. He could smell the cinnamon and fresh-baked bread drifting in the sultry breeze.

On top of the blacktop in the church parking lot, Mrs. Lawrence had brought them a gallon of water and several glasses of her all-too-sweet lemonade. But the thirst Luke had couldn't be filled with water.

He wanted another chance to pull Bridget Wilson in his arms and kiss her so silly she wouldn't keep running from him. She showed up at practice and helped as he asked her, but when he drew close, she shied away. Maybe Bridget didn't feel the way he did, but her side long glances said she did. And he noticed.

"Hey man, what do you say we head down into the church basement for a breather and see if we can't get Pete's mother-in-law to give up one of those cinnamon treats in the oven?"

"I imagine it's hotter down there than it is up here," Sam chimed in.

Luke lifted his hat and swiped the sweat across his forehead with his arm. He was not much good with his arms as
slick with sweat as his face. He grunted as Sam tilted his head.
"There's air conditioning down at the diner. I heard Gwen say
they were serving cold hoagies today with her and Curt
helping with the food prep for the festival."

"Bring me back two, would you?" Luke reached for his
wallet. "And a gallon of iced tea."

Pete clamped him on the shoulder. "I've got this man. I
owe you for the grill."

Luke frowned. Slipping his wallet in his pocket. "I don't
remember saying it had a price on it."

"Then let a man buy his friend lunch." Pete put down the
wrench they used to tighten the bolts to hold the counter up in
front of the booth. "You sure you're not coming? It's hot out
here. Take a break."

"I've got one more tent to raise, and then I'll call it a day."
Luke glanced over at his truck. He told Bridget he would help
her set up the booth this evening after practice with the kids,
but he lied. Luke had everything on the back of his truck to
raise the vendor tent. He had Jim Hastings order from the
hardware store online for him.

He wanted to surprise her. He'd watched her over the past
few days, sitting with Lizzy and Angie while he pulled parts
and fixed machines for folk. She kept them busy with a pile of
fabric and ribbon. He'd seen her at night with the lights still
on in the RV and the soft hum of her sewing machine. He
guessed that's what she'd had in the box she'd held onto when
he first found her.

"Have lunch with us, Luke." Sam hitched his thumb
toward Pete, waiting for him. "I'll help you when we get
back."

"Don't you have work on the farm?" Luke asked.

"There's always work at the farm. Dad's slopped the hogs

by now, and he said he could bring Bryson in later for practice."

Bryson was Sam's son. Like most of them, Sam had left after high school to make a life elsewhere. Then a few years later, Sam returned to raise his son. Being a single father wasn't always easy. Luke felt for him. He'd seen his sister, Lisa, struggle. But Lisa's struggles differed from Sam's. He often wondered if Sam and Lisa would connect and support each other, but they'd never been friends in school. Lisa was a few years younger than Sam, and her heart was still bruised from her past.

Luke shook his head. "I appreciate the offer, but I want to get this done so I can surprise Bridget. You understand?"

"Oh, I understand." Sam lifted his hat and grinned.

Luke spotted Pastor Lawrence coming out of the church as Sam waved and took off with Pete for lunch.

"You're all doing a fine job putting this all together. I can't say how much we appreciate everyone helping." A tall, slim man, Pastor Lawrence, looked over the booth they'd assembled.

"No need." Luke moved over to his truck. He parked it near the space Bridget had rented for her booth. He opened the tailgate and pulled the tent out.

"I've been meaning to come over to the farm. With the festival, it's been busy, and I wanted to introduce myself to your guest properly. I've noticed she's been coming to church with you on Sundays."

Luke took a deep breath. He'd seen this coming, didn't know when to expect it, and continued doing what he needed to be done. "Yep. Take her to visit my mom, too. She looks forward to seeing her."

Pastor Lawrence helped with taking off the covering of the tent. It was simple enough, unzip, pull off, then the tent would spread out and push up like the canopy it was built to be. He had cement blocks for weight around the legs, and it came with sides to put on at night for closing.

"Bridget, right? She seems like a woman of God's heart."

Luke could hear the sermon rising in his mind, the lecture, and the muscle in his jaw tightened. Pastor Lawrence had a right to be curious. He made a point of getting to know all those in the congregation.

"She is." Luke and Bridget had spent a lot of time together, and even though he didn't know everything about her, the things they shared during their evening talks over supper had been enough for him. Homeless or not, he decided, he would have felt the same about her.

With the tent up and Luke going around and locking in the sides so they'd stand, Pastor Lawrence set down the last of the cement blocks for him. "Luke, I guess I'm gonna be real honest with you. I've known you since you were a teenager, and Lisa, too."

Luke went to his truck and pulled out the two tables he borrowed from the old schoolhouse when the church had its own private academy. "Lisa came to you."

"Well, you can imagine. She had some concerns. You can't blame her for feeling the way she does."

"Before you say another word, Pastor, I think you should know I have no intention of sending Bridget away."

"You have feelings for her." Pastor Lawrence watched as Luke set up the tables.

He needed to do something. Luke would never admit what he held inside him. He told a girl once he loved her, and she laughed at him. As did the entire student body in high school his senior year. He wasn't looking to repeat the experience.

"You're like your father, Luke. He was a good man. He also knew he couldn't fix everything. I know your intentions are good."

"She's not hurting anyone out there. I'm not taking her to

a shelter. She belongs here, in this town." And, he almost confessed, she belonged with him. His heart skipped a beat.

When had she become more special to him than a friend?

Dear Lord, Luke realized. He loved Bridget Wilson.

"I couldn't agree more," Pastor Lawrence said. "But some folks in town might see this as not too proper for a single gal living out in your barn."

"RV," Luke said.

"RV," Pastor Lawrence continued. "Marlene's got rooms at her place. She said the girls come in the library a time or two. She's willing to put her up there while she gets on her feet and finds a place of her own."

"She's got a place." Luke slammed the tailgate up. "She's got a job. I don't care what others think."

Pastor Lawrence pulled out a handkerchief and dabbed at the sweat on his forehead. "What does she think?"

Luke shrugged.

"Maybe you should ask her." Pastor Lawrence tilted his head. Bridget stood with two hoagies and a pint of iced tea in the other.

His chest grew tight, and Pastor Lawrence waved at Bridget. "It's good to see you again, Bridget."

She frowned, eyes following as Pastor Lawrence escaped inside the cool building. As she approached, a scowl deepened on her face. Her hair was pulled into a ponytail, and her shoulders tinged pink from being out in the sun too long.

"What was that about?"

Her eyes, filled with curiosity and distrust, squeezed at his gut. How was he going to tell her he loved her?

Then she shoved the hoagies and the iced tea at him, walking past him to the tent. "You didn't wait for me."

Her accusation stung.

"I thought I would be nice and surprise you."

Her glare softened, and he thought he saw a hint of a

smile. She glanced over her shoulder at him. He braced for her to snap at him, but she said, "Thank you."

He held out one hoagy. "I ordered one for you."

"There is a shady spot around front." She waited for him on the steps where the shadow of the morning sun beat away the heat.

He handed her the hoagie. "It's nice not having the girls around for a bit."

"You miss them." She leaned back against the brick and opened the wrappings.

"You get used to them."

That brought a twinkle in her eyes. "Maybe someday you'll have a family of your own."

"Someday."

"What did you say to Pastor Lawrence?" she asked.

"That I enjoyed having you around." And when he leaned against the wall of the front of the church, her cheeks matched the pink of her shoulders.

13

Late in the afternoon, Luke loaded Bridget's bike on the back of his truck. He went up to the house to take Lizzy and Angie to their mother. Later, he promised to help load Bridget's things for their booth at the festival, which officially started tomorrow evening and ran through the weekend.

He'd seemed more closed up than usual, and she couldn't help wondering if it had something to do with earlier.

Lisa brought the girls to the ball field, and Lizzy sat beside Bridget, having spent the day with her grandparents. Lisa stood off to the side of the home team dugout, her arms crossed. Luke scowled.

It was none of her business, but she felt their discussion included bits about her. Lisa would nod in her direction, and her hands would wave and point.

Lizzy watched. Her little lips were turned down in a frown. "We had to stay with our grandparents today."

"Did you have fun?" Bridget asked, trying to ignore the sinking feeling in her stomach at the sound of Lisa's high-pitched voice on this side of where they stood. The kids continued to play as usual.

"I drew a picture, and Angie wrote a letter to Daddy.

Grandma Shaw is going to send it with her next care package."

"She must miss him a lot."

Lizzy shrugged. "Momma says she doesn't care if Daddy ever comes back. She said he lost his mind and didn't think about us."

"I'm sure that's not what your mom means."

Lizzy's innocent words still burned in her gut long after Luke brought them home. Not once had Bridget's grandmother ever said a bad thing about where Bridget came from. Her mother hadn't forgotten her, but she recognized she wasn't in a good place to raise a child. Bridget prayed Lizzy's mother got the help she needed. All the while, she had a good life with Granny. One day, she prayed her mother would return so she could at least tell her.

She gave Lizzy and Angie the biggest hugs before they headed across the road.

She saved half her hoagie from lunch for supper, and she'd smuggled half an apple pie in the truck under Angie's doll blanket to surprise Luke with for supper.

He came and ate with her every night. Some evenings after the kids went home from practice, he took her to the diner or up to his place in the house's basement.

She stood outside the RV, thinking she would call it a night, even though the sun hadn't gone down.

"It's the best part of the day," Luke said, coming up behind her.

"I was just thinking it's been a long day, and maybe I'd call it a day." She headed to her RV.

"Not yet." Luke said, "I think we should talk."

"Talk?" She didn't like that word. This had to do with Lisa, with her, and Luke. How long had she been here? A few weeks? It felt longer. Her heart squeezed with Anne's friendship, Luke, and the girls. What had she expected? To stay here?

It was never the goal.

"Why don't we go for a ride?" He looked at her, his eyes sincere. His face was set on whatever he had planned.

"Do I get a few minutes to gather my stuff?"

Luke's eyes bulged as if someone had slugged him. "Your stuff? No." He frowned. "We're not taking the truck. Not tonight. We'll take your stuff to the church tomorrow."

"So ... what, you take me on a farewell date and bye-bye Bridget in the morning?" She bit the inside of her mouth from letting her true hurt show.

"I'm trying to take you out in the field and put you on a horse, woman, to go for a ride in the sunset." Luke huffed.

"Oh." She looked at him, the unsettled part inside her working itself back together. "A horseback ride."

"I said I'd get you on a horse. Tonight's the perfect night." He held his hand out to her.

"That's what you want to talk about?"

He confused her. Her heart slowed from its prior rapid beat. She placed her hand in his. Her fingers trembled as he entwined his between hers and gave a gentle squeeze. "No." He tugged her closer to him. She watched his lips moving, heard his words, and couldn't move an inch as he drew closer. Her eyes were still on his mouth as it hovered over hers, gently brushing her lips and murmuring, "I think we need to talk about this."

She let her lips do the talking for her. Luke wrapped his arms around her waist and brought her closer. Her arms around his neck, she kissed him back. He wanted her. He wasn't asking her to leave, or was he?

Bye-bye, Bridget, she tensed.

"Bridget?" Luke said.

"I don't think we should do this, Luke." She slid her hands down from around his neck. "Your sister —"

"Will get over it." Luke tightened his hold. He brought his mouth down again when she turned her face. He kissed her cheek. He trailed kisses to her ear. "Go on a ride with me tonight?"

Riding atop a horse or letting Luke keep kissing her, Bridget couldn't decide which she feared more. She gave in to the riding. "Just this once."

Somehow falling off a horse didn't seem like it would hurt as much as her heart when Luke realized she wasn't worth keeping around.

Hand in hand, they walked out to the field. Luke put a bridle over his shoulder. "Isn't there a saddle or something?"

"Not this time."

She watched while he coaxed Romeo to him. He slid the bridle over the horse's head, and the gelding champed at the bit. With the reins draped to the ground, the horse stood. "He's trained to stand until his reins are picked up."

Bridget shook her head. This had been a bad idea. Maybe she'd go back to kissing Luke and pull out that apple pie she had for him in the RV. He seemed to read her mind when he hooked his arm around her waist. "I'll give you a leg up. Then I'll hop on behind you."

She gave Romeo a skeptical look. "Hey Romeo, buddy old pal. Just gonna get a leg up and sit on you, if that's okay."

Luke kissed her on her temple. "Relax. I've got you both. You'll be fine. I'm right here."

"If that is supposed to make me feel better, it doesn't." Bridget tried to calm down and relax as Luke told her. "No, take hold of his mane here." Luke took her hands and had her grasp the end of Romeo's mane nearest the top of his shoulders. She smoothed down his hair and whispered. "Good boy, Romeo. Good boy to stand while the crazy man puts me on your back."

Luke chuckled. "Easy now." Romeo sidestepped a little, and she gulped. Her heart was about to jump into her throat. "He can sense your fear." Luke put her hand on Romeo's back at the mane. "Take his mane in your hand."

"Won't this hurt him?" Won't this hurt me? It seemed like a long way up and a long way to tumble down on the other side.

Misty kept her distance, the mare's head up, alert. She nickered, even though Bridget didn't find it encouraging.

"Now, I'm going to cup my hands like this." Luke put his hands together and bent. "Put your left foot here, and when I lift you, lift your right leg up and around the horse."

Romeo seemed to agree this wouldn't work. His ears went back, flat against his head. "Thanks for the confidence," Bridget said.

"You can do this. Leg up. Ready?"

No, not really. Her heart seemed stuck halfway up her chest and beating wildly.

Luke stepped in front of her, smacked a good old mind-sapping kiss on her lips, and before she could react, her foot was in his hands, and her other leg was swinging up over the horse. She blinked. She was on top of Romeo. "Good girl." He patted her leg.

Misty came up beside her as if to say, *you traitor* then spun around and kicked both hind legs in her direction, racing a distance away.

Luke tapped Bridget's thigh to get her attention. "I'm going to walk you over by the old truck parked on the other side of the hill. Then I'll get on. It'll make it easier for all of us."

"Why aren't you riding, Misty?" As Luke took Romeo's reins, the horse started moving beneath her. Bridget yelped and fisted her hand into the mane more tightly. She slid, but Luke's hand on her hip kept her from falling.

"Tighten your legs around him a little but be careful you don't put your heels in him or kick him," Luke said.

"What happens if I do?" She kept her eyes locked on Luke, and he flipped the reins up around Romeo's neck so they crisscrossed at her hands. When she had more of a grip on her seat and the horse's walking motion, Luke moved up by Romeo's head.

"I won't be able to hold him back from taking off," Luke said, and Bridget kept her heels from the horse's side. He led her away through the field. Slowly, she relaxed, feeling the motion of the horse beneath her.

At the truck, she scooted up closer to the mane at the place Luke called the 'withers' as Romeo danced a little when he got on behind her.

He reached around her, one hand holding the reins, the other around her waist. She leaned back against him, keeping a hold on the mane. She didn't trust for a minute Romeo wouldn't take off and leave them both planted faces first in the grass.

"Not so bad, is it?" Luke asked.

"Don't push your luck, cowboy," she teased.

Alongside them, Misty walked and followed. Several times the mare pressed her nose over to their legs, and Bridget soon felt comfortable enough to release the hold of one of her hands on Romeo's mane to reach over and pat Misty.

They rode through the middle of the field, headed at an angle toward the setting sun. At the top of a slope, the sun looked to sink at its lowest. Bridget sighed. If she never got on a horse again, it was worth it for this moment. Her head rested against Luke's shoulder. He laid his cheek alongside hers. "You don't see sunsets like this in the city."

Or ride horseback with handsome cowboys who spend their time looking after their nieces or giving stuff to folks who need it, or visiting their ailing mother every Sunday.

"It's beautiful." Through the trees, the sky was as far as one could see. No, there was nothing like it in all the world.

"I figured you'd like it."

She reached her free hand back to cover the one around her waist. She pushed her fingers between his, the intimate act sending a flush up her neck.

Bridget's heart swelled larger in love with Luke Myers.

"Luke." She bit her lip, about to tell him, then said, "There's half an apple pie of Gwen's in my RV waiting for you if you can get me back to the barn in one piece."

Luke tightened his arm around her, and his deep chuckle vibrated against her should blades. He kissed her cheek and said, "You know the way to a man's heart."

14

Luke never had a chance to fully down his first cup of coffee as Lisa stormed into the milk house in a huff. "The girls are in the barn. You can drop them off with Mrs. Shaw before you head out. She said after eight is fine."

"Why can't they stay here?" Luke blinked, still trying to get the sleep out of his eyes. He tapped his head with his palm, thinking something must have got disconnected.

"There's not enough room in your truck for Sonya and Jimmy with the girls along."

Luke took a long swig of his coffee. "Sonya and Jimmy are coming home today?"

Lisa spread out her arms. "I told you yesterday."

"Before or after you lecture me on having Bridget here?" Luke held onto his coffee cup. "You know, Pastor Lawrence came to see me, Lisa."

"Somebody has to speak some sense in your head. You can load her up and drop her off at the shelter on your way to Lexington."

Luke put down his coffee, and the hot liquid splashed over his hand, not that he felt it. Six o'clock in the morning, and already, his blood had been set on boiling. He fixed his stare on Lisa. "Now you listen here, little sister. I don't know what's gotten into you lately, but Bridget is staying here, and you'd best get used to it."

Lisa crossed her arms. "You like her, don't you?"

Luke returned her glare.

"Oh, Luke, please tell me you haven't fallen in love with that girl. You took her riding last night, didn't you? That's Doug's horse."

"At least you remember his name."

Lisa paled. "Of course, I know his name, which is why I'm telling you now to get rid of this girl. I've seen her type. She'll suck you dry for what she can, and at the first opportunity, back to the city, she'll go. People ain't like us, Luke. Not everybody holds to their roots. She'll break your heart, then you'll end up here pining over her, and she won't care."

"Maybe some people just need to find their roots before they can plant them." Luke wiped the coffee up with a rag by the table.

"You're just like Dad. No sense in trying to talk to you. We both know this is home. This is where our hearts are. She'll miss the city, you'll see, and she'll go right on back there."

"You know if you gave her a chance, got to know her like the other folk. She might not seem so bad to you."

"I don't have time for this, Luke. I told Sonya you'd be around to pick her and Jimmy up this afternoon. You know she doesn't have a car out there. And if you're smart, you'll pack up that woman and drop her off on your way. Everyone figured you'd be dating Sonya with the way you two get along so well."

"We like baseball. That's about it."

"And your city girl? What's she like?" Lisa glanced behind her, hearing the girls whispering and coming around the doorway.

Apple pie, fixing things, and making her way. "We're more alike than you'd think."

Lisa scowled. "Don't forget Sonya today. She and Jimmy are counting on you." Then she turned and addressed the two girls standing outside the door. "Be good for Uncle Luke and mind your manners with Granny Shaw, you hear?"

Both girls nodded and took off as they heard the door on the old camper snap shut. "Bridget!"

Lisa walked to her car, got in, and sat there for a moment. Luke watched as she pulled away and headed down the road. He poured another cup of coffee and made a quick phone call while the girls hugged and said good morning to Bridget.

He met her inside the barn with a cup of coffee in each hand. She had on a pair of cut-off shorts and a paint-splattered T-shirt. She reached for the coffee, and he held it out of her reach. "Good morning, Bridget."

She smiled, leaning in to kiss him on the cheek and snatch his cup of coffee. She took a sip, fluttering her lashes over the rim, and said, "Morning, Luke."

Lizzy came skipping around them. "Luke and Brig-It up in a tree —"

"Now, you stop that." Luke waved her away, and Angie stood giggling.

Bridget turned pink. He liked that look on her. "It's too early in the morning for all your energy, Lizzy."

"What are we doing today?" Lizzy asked.

Angie shook her head. "Momma said we're going to Grandma's."

"I don't want to go. I want to stay here and help Brig-It. We need to make more stuff."

"Not today." Bridget ran her hand over Lizzy's hair. "I've got to get things set up at the festival starting this evening. How about I do your hair, and I'll put one of those pretty ribbons in it we made the other day."

"But don't you need to sell them?" Angie asked, her voice just as shy as she was.

"Not these. I made these just for you girls." Bridget tilted her head toward the camper. "We'll be in there if you need us."

"Why don't you girls run ahead? I need to talk to Bridget about something first," Luke said.

"You gonna ask her to marry you? Cause I don't want to miss that." Lizzy rushed up between them.

Bridget almost dropped her coffee cup, and Luke reached out to catch it if she let go.

"Not today, pumpkin. Go on, wait for Bridget at the camper. We've got a busy morning ahead."

"Will you do my hair, too?"

"Of course," Bridget said, then looked at Luke. "What's up?"

Luke walked out ahead of her, watching Lizzy and Angie go to the old RV camper. "I've had something come up today, so I cannot help you set up like we figured."

Bridget frowned. "Is everything okay?"

Luke took a big gulp of his coffee. The right thing to do would be to tell Bridget where he was going and why, but Lisa's words whittled away at him. What if she wanted to go to? What if she wanted to stay in the city?

He took her hand. "Nothing to worry about. I've got to do a favor for a friend. I'm not sure what time I'll get back. Anne and Pete said they'd give you a hand setting up. I'm sorry, Bridget. I got to go do this."

She wrapped her arms around him. "I know. You're a good friend."

Luke lifted her chin. "I'm your friend, Bridget. Not like the other friends you've had in the past."

"No, Luke Myers, you're nothing like any friend I've ever had. You're more."

He could stand there, staring at those eyes all morning. Lizzy shouted. "Kiss her already! We got to git our hair done!"

Luke closed his eyes and shook his head. In his arms,

Bridget laughed. She gave him a nudge. "Yeah, Uncle Luke, kiss me already. We got to get our hair done. And the sooner you go, you can get right on back here, so you don't miss the first game."

Luke groaned. He had almost forgotten about the baseball game. He needed to hightail it out of there if he was to return by four o'clock for the game. "You're going to be there, right?"

"I thought that's why you made me your assistant, so I'd have to be there."

"You've figured me out." Luke leaned in. "Best, give me a kiss and maybe one for the road."

Bridget laughed again. He liked her laugh. He liked her better with her held tight in his arms. His lips pressed with hers, the taste of coffee and creamer between them.

"Did she say yes?" Lizzy raced, pushing between them.

"Oh, Lizzy, stop it." Angie was behind her, taking her sister's hand and pulling her away.

"Say yes to what?" Bridget glanced over at her.

"She's been watching too many of those dress shows with Momma," Angie said.

"Oh." Bridget tensed. She pulled away from Luke. Reluctant, he took the empty cup of coffee from her hand. "Well, we best get your hair done for the day."

"Can I get a braid?" Angie asked.

"You gonna marry Uncle Luke?" Lizzy asked.

Bridget's face paled. She glanced between Luke and Lizzy.

"Lizzy," Luke said, his voice stern.

"Well?" Lizzy huffed. "Momma says no kissing unless you're married."

Bridget wrapped her arm around Lizzy. "Your momma's right." Bridget beamed at Luke. She pointed her finger. "No more kissing, you hear?"

"Not until we're married," he agreed. Bridget's smile went flat. Her eyes became serious. "Until we're married and not a day sooner."

Then her eyes danced with mischief, and she turned away with the girls. Lizzy asked various questions, and Bridget answered, "Maybe someday."

Luke finished loading Bridget's masterpieces on the bed of his truck. He dropped them off at Bridget's tent at the church, confident no one would disturb them. When he returned for the girls, they had braids and ribbons in their hair.

Bridget waved at him as he left, and the further he drove away from her, the heavier the guilt twisted his gut. He couldn't take a chance on the one time Lisa might be right. Lord forgive him, if Bridget wanted to leave, she should go, but little Lizzy had been right. He couldn't keep kissing Bridget without telling her how he felt. She deserved to have a home, people who loved her, and a family. And he wanted to be that man to give them to her.

15

It started sprinkling rain mid-morning. Anne closed the shop early to help Bridget finish setting up her booth. She sold all four of the macrame lawn chairs to other vendors within the first hour of putting them out at the front of the booth.

"It's a good thing you kept one of those for yourself." Anne sorted out the patchwork tote bags and hung them off a coat stand Luke had fashioned from an old barn door with a bench at the bottom. "You'll have to charge more in the future."

"And here I thought people wouldn't pay as much for things as they do in the city." Bridget rearranged the baler twine wreaths tied with red gingham bows and the rusted old cogs she had made into candle holders. She put them on the far side, closest to the woman selling candles.

"Too bad you don't have more."

"There's one I started in the barn, but I didn't have time to finish it. The girls and I searched, and we found all that could be salvaged."

Then Anne gave her a look, and Bridget asked, "What?"

Anne waved her hand. "I can see why Luke is taken with you. You're a woman of his own heart, fixing things, repurposing it. Pete said Luke's been getting more done with you keeping the girls occupied. Where are they? I thought they'd be with you."

"They're with the Shaws. I know Lizzy loves going over there."

Her heart sank a little deeper each time she thought of the girls, not knowing their father. She never knew her father, so she prayed for them each night. She dreamed her father would show up if only to meet him. For Lizzy and Angie's sakes, she hoped with all her heart their daddy was safe and would come home to them one day.

"Let's hope Luke doesn't get too held up, or he might not make it in time for the kid's game. He was worried you'd have no one to help you today."

"He's kind like that." Reserved as Luke could be, she had started to appreciate his pillar of respecting other people's privacy. She watched him tear things apart and drive out through the fields to get parts of machines, never charging what it most likely was worth. Luke was always content to help someone within their means. She realized he'd done the same for her, and her stomach fluttered.

Anne gave her an amused look. "What?"

"Oh, honey, you've got it bad." Anne laughed.

"I do not." Bridget fussed over moving one thing this way, another that. Thanks to Luke's handiwork and her and the girls' adventures through the fields of junk beyond the hill, she'd created many things for her booth in such a short time.

Small things she and the girls made, like wreaths and wall decor. Luke had done the bigger stuff, the coat hanger, the planters, cubes, and trunks made from lockers and old metal desks for storage and coffee tables.

She asked Anne's advice after researching their items online for prices but wanting to stay within a reasonable range for the small-town economy. The idea was to find a new home for it and make a few dollars while she did it.

Oh, of course, Luke liked her. They were partners—sort of.

"You made more!" Anne exclaimed, taking the lid off a box of hair barrettes and bands. "You have any left. You bring them down to the shop. I don't have any left from the ones you brought the other day."

"You can take some of them now."

Anne put them down, arranging them at the front of the booth. "The shop is closed until Monday if you don't have any left you'll have to make more. You working on that online site?"

"Little by little." The truth was, she'd stepped away from the computer Luke set up for her and used the one at the library to set up Luke's new website. But she'd sent an email to Shelby, her gut changing from a flutter to tightening as she hadn't heard back from her 'friend.' She'd promised to send what she owed Shelby for the past due rent in payments. Pastor Lawrence had spoken about making things right in one's heart and facing the consequences of actions. She didn't want the burden of owing Shelby weighing on her heart as she made a future — one she was praying included Luke.

"All done." Anne grinned, then tilted her head. "You know, Pete said he never thought he'd see the day Luke got smitten by a woman. All I have to say is I'm glad it's you."

"Thanks, Anne. I don't know where this is gonna go. I don't even know if I'll be staying here. I can't live in Luke's RV forever, but I'm grateful for the time I have here."

Anne reached over and hugged her. At first, Bridget didn't know what to do. Not many people hugged her, except maybe Luke these days. Slowly she relaxed and hugged Anne back. "I've got something I need to take care of. Would you mind watching the booth for a few minutes while I run down the street to the bank?"

"Sure thing. Did Luke say where he was going?"

"No. Just that he had to get back before the game."

Bridget gathered her purse. "I'll grab us a cinnamon bun from the church booth."

Heading down the street, Bridget waved to Marge and Maeve, sitting at a table with used books for sale from the library. She walked to the bank, and Lisa and another woman stood at the counter. Bridget waited, thankful Lisa had a customer, and moved to another teller, Brenda.

Bridget recognized her from the barbecue at Anne and Pete's house. Brenda asked, "Can I help you?"

Bridget pulled out her wallet and a few dollars she'd earned this past week selling things and helping Anne. She slid the money toward Brenda. "I'd like to put half in my account and the other half as a money order, please."

Bridget kept her eyes on Brenda as Lisa's customer stepped away, and Bridget felt Lisa looking at her. She turned to shield herself from seeing Lisa, uncomfortable. Coming into contact with Lisa's ice-ray stare had been one reason she'd been putting it off since Luke had brought her in and helped her set up an account.

"Sure thing." Brenda smiled. Her short dark hair curled around her chin as she filled out the deposit slip and counted Bridget's money.

"Brenda." Lisa stepped over behind the woman. "We don't do money orders. She'll have to go to the post office."

"Oh, that's right." Brenda smiled apologetically. Bridget shifted, holding onto the strap of her purse. "We stopped doing money orders last month."

Lisa nodded and returned to her teller station. Another customer walked into the bank, and Lisa greeted them.

Brenda glanced at Lisa and then slid Bridget's deposit slip back. "Just let me check something." Brenda kept her hand on the other half of Bridget's money.

Bridget shrugged. She bit her lip, wanting to get to her booth again. Luke had given her enough change for the booth. She could deal with Lisa not liking her. Not that she could figure out why, but living in the city, she understood people didn't always like each other. In time, she hoped she and Lisa could establish some type of comfort zone for Luke's sake.

"Oh, yes. That's what I was looking for." Brenda beamed. "I can write you a cashier's check if you'd like."

"How much will that cost?" Bridget asked.

"Nothing. It's included in your checking account. You're the second level above basic. It includes free cashier checks."

"Oh, okay." Luke Myers. Bridget sighed. What was she gonna do with him? Then a piece of her heart said she would love him.

"Who would you like me to make it out to?"

"Um ... Shelby Benson, and if you could print 'rent' in the memo, I'd appreciate it."

She waited while Brenda prepared her to check. Behind her, Lisa spoke with her customer. "Going to the game this evening, Mike?"

"Sure thing. Luke's doing a good job with those kids. Shame what happened with Jimmy. Miss seeing him and Sonya down at the ballpark."

"You should see them tonight. Luke went to get them. You know how close they are and how much Luke thinks of them," Lisa said.

Bridget's hand reached out and held onto the counter. Luke went to get Sonya. That's why he'd gone to Lexington the day she met him. Lexington. Her heart pounded. Luke went to Lexington and didn't tell her.

About to whirl around and ask Lisa, Brenda came with Bridget's check. "Just need you to read it over and make sure it's all good."

Bridget hurried and read it. "It's fine."

Her heart and her brain are racing against each other. Why would he go and not tell her why he went? She tried to calm down. Luke would have said. He would have told her.

It's not a big deal, she assured herself. So what if Luke went to get the woman and the boy? He'd told her about Jimmy, hadn't he?

Knowing Luke, it was another one of his acts of kindness to help someone.

Bridget reached for the check. "One minute. Lisa, can you sign this for me?" Brenda said. "Sorry, I need a second signature on the check to validate it."

When Lisa finished with Mike, she came over. Brenda handed her the check, and Lisa read it over. Her brow raised, but other than that, Luke's sister didn't say a word. She signed the check and handed it to Brenda with a smile.

"Here you go."

Bridget took the check. She forced herself to walk out of the bank slowly. The wave of heat from outside the air-conditioned building flushed her cheek. Numbly she walked to the post office, mailed the check to her old residence, and returned to Anne.

"You okay?" Anne asked. "It looks like the heat is getting to you. Maybe I'll grab us some water over in the church from the ladies in the kitchen."

Bridget put her purse under her booth table and sank into the chair. Anne stood next to her. "I know where Luke went."

"Where's that?"

"Lexington, to pick up the woman and her son." Bridget glanced up at Anne. She didn't know whether to be hurt, shocked, or angry, but a low burn started in her gut. Why hadn't Luke told her that's where he was going?

"Makes sense. Sonya rode up in the ambulance and didn't leave, so she had no car there. It's kind of Luke to go get her."

"I suppose it is."

Anne crossed her arms. "I know it is. Just like I know this has Lisa written all over it. Don't think for a moment that Sonya's brother or father wouldn't have gone for her and

Jimmy. Lisa put him up to it. She's been trying to pair them together for a while now."

"Then I came along and messed things up."

"You messed nothing up. If Luke liked Sonya, they would have gone out long ago. They're friends. You belong here, Bridget, and you belong with Luke. Understand?" Anne put her hands on her hips, not about to take no for an answer.

"I've got to go check in with the boys. They're at my mom's. I'll be back soon. You get those thoughts out of your head. Don't let Lisa win. Remember what Pastor Lawrence said,' God doesn't make mistakes.' Luke found you and brought you here for a reason. You two belong together."

Bridget tried to put on her best smile. Anne's words were a balm to her bruised heart. Of course, why would Luke kiss her if he liked someone else? For pity's sake, they weren't in grade school anymore. Her life before this seemed like one unfortunate event after another until she came here. Until she met Luke.

Oh Lord, she thought. *I want to stay here and be with Luke. I want to believe. Help me believe.*

Then a few women came to check out her booth. Bridget put those feelings in a pocket where she could pull them out later.

16

Traffic getting out of Lexington could have been better. Jimmy sat between him and Sonya, the boy's head on his mother's shoulder. He didn't know why Lisa would put him up to this when she knew all he had was his truck. The kid needed to be in the backseat, leaning back and resting for the trip home. And home he wouldn't be for very long, as he still had appointments and surgeries in the future.

It made Luke's hand tighten on the wheel. Jimmy laid his head against his mother, Luke prayed the kid made it through the ride without getting sick. As pale as the poor boy looked, he should still be at the hospital. Luke had half a mind to turn around and take him back, but the traffic trapped him into going southwest, and there was no place to get out of the lane.

He tapped his fingers on the steering wheel. Sonya brushed her hand over Jimmy's hair. "You think we'll make the game in time?"

"Depends on this traffic." Friday afternoon, and everyone headed out of the city for an early weekend. He tried only to think nice things about his sister, and Lord help him, he mulled over a few kind choice words when he saw her.

"It means a lot you came for us. Means a lot to Jimmy," Sonya said.

"You sure he's gonna be up to the game?" Luke asked, glancing over at Jimmy, asleep against his mother.

"He won't be able to play again until next summer, but he's been missing the kids. He's been looking forward to watching them play. I promised he could be our scorekeeper, and help us out, so he still feels part of the team since he can't play."

Luke nodded. He hadn't accounted for Sonya stepping in again to help. With it being July, the all-star games were almost over, and his team had just these games during the festival before the season ended. Sonya had been one of the moms most eager to assist with helping the kids and volunteering to be his assistant coach. "It might be too much for him. And with him needing you, it's okay. Bridget's been helping me out. She's done good with the kids and keeping the scorebook in order."

"Bridget? Is that the woman Lisa says is staying in your Daddy's old RV? By the way, Lisa talked. I thought she'd be gone by now."

Luke tightened his hands on the steering wheel. "No, she's not." He couldn't admit right then he didn't want her to either.

"Oh," was all Sonya said, and then planted a kiss on Jimmy's unruly crown of hair. "I'm sure she'll understand, not being from here."

They drove the rest of the way to Hidden Hills in quiet. Luke rehearsed in his head what he wanted to say to Bridget. Thinking of what he wouldn't say to his sister and how he didn't want to disappoint a kid and a friend.

The traffic held them up by twenty minutes, and when he got to the ball field, the kids had just finished the national anthem. Bridget stood by the dugout, and little Lizzy had a team hat on, standing beside her. Lisa sat and spoke on the bleachers, her smile growing wider than before when she spotted Luke and Sonya. Jimmy had trouble walking fast and still should have been in the hospital or home, in Luke's opinion.

The kid didn't weigh much, so Luke swung him up in his arms and carried him to the dugout. Bridget turned, a flood of relief in those pretty eyes of hers. She moved out of the way for him to take Jimmy inside. "I was worried you wouldn't make it in time."

"Traffic." He grunted, finding a spot for Jimmy on the bench inside where it was cool from the lingering heat. Lizzy skipped after him, happy to see an old friend. As he came out of the dugout, Sonya approached Bridget. "You must be Bridget. I'm Sonya. Thanks so much for covering for me until I got here." Sonya held out her hand, but when Bridget extended to shake, Sonya took the scorebook from her instead.

"Jimmy's gonna keep score. You understand, right? He's been so excited to get here."

A man across the way waved and shouted to Sonya. She waved and shouted back to give them a minute, and they could play baseball. He gave her a thumbs up.

Luke walked out and went to put his arm around Bridget when she stepped away. "Of course. Have a good game."

The glance she gave him before she hurried away sliced his heart. "Bridget."

"Don't worry about me. You've got a game to coach."

Sonya stood before him when he went to follow Bridget out around the dugout. "Looks like we're three hitters in already." Then Sonya started shouting for the kids to change positions on the field.

Luke held up his hand. "I've got this. You stick close to Jimmy."

He turned his hat around, switched to coaching mode, and couldn't help glancing around every so often for Bridget. He spotted her near Anne. At the top of the third inning, his kids were down by three runs and kept the encouragement coming.

Sonya pushed them like she always did but stuck close to Jimmy. By the end of the sixth inning, they were too far behind to catch up. Even with their great effort in the seventh, his kids lost. He glanced around the crowd, but no Bridget.

He directed the kids and their parents up to the church parking lot, where he got the kids ice cream for their efforts. He got one for Bridget, headed over to her booth, and found Anne.

"Have you seen Bridget?" he asked.

Anne stood at her booth while Pete kept the boys from getting ice cream drips over everything. "She helped Marge carry some things down to her place. She shouldn't be long."

"I can stay here and help her close things up when she returns," Luke said. He looked out across the parking lot. Over half the town mingled and hung out at different spots. Sonya fussed over Jimmy while Angie and Lizzy played with the kids in the church playground. Several had taken their cones and sat on the roundabout.

"You have a nice night?" Anne said.

He watched the family walk away, headed to the play-ground for the boys to run off all that sugar energy before bed.

Soon, Bridget returned. She wore the same pair of denim shorts and a baseball T-shirt he had seen her in earlier. With her hair in a ponytail and her cheeks flushed, he wanted to kiss her.

"I got you ice cream, but it melted, so I gave it away. I can get you another if you don't mind waiting while I stand in line."

Her expression was hard to read. She shook her head. "No, thank you."

"I can see if they've got some pie left?" He moved closer as she retreated inside the booth.

"I'm not hungry." She picked up and rearranged things on the table. He followed her.

"Do good today?" He couldn't tell, not knowing how much she had to start with.

She shrugged.

"Something wrong?" he asked.

Bridget sighed. "It's just been a long day. I'm ready to go home."

With that, he could agree. Luke gave her a nudge. "Let's close this up and head to the farm."

Luke helped Bridget, and they quickly put up the tent sides and closed things up. When he tried to slip his hand into hers, she stuck them in her pockets. In the truck, she watched out the window. Quiet and reserved.

Back at the barn, he walked her to the RV. "It's too dark to ride tonight, but we could go up on the hill and count the stars."

She leaned against him, wrapped her arms around him. "I'm too tired. I'd fall asleep on the hill."

"I could carry you." And as he hoped, he heard a muffled laugh.

"It's gonna rain again tomorrow. I need to get up early. I sold all the chairs." She yawned. "And the hair bows."

"Bridget." He didn't want to talk about chairs or hair bows. He bent his head, pressed his cheek against hers. "Thank you for being so understanding about today."

Her arms fell away from him, and she stepped away. "Sure thing. Goodnight, Luke."

He watched her go inside, then walked across the road and up to the house. Lisa was in the kitchen, and he walked around the house to the basement door of his place.

He spent part of the night reading various passages, none comforting his troubled mind. He prayed this feeling of uncertainty would go away and the things he was worried about would be for not. He should have told her he loved her.

Maybe then she would have wrapped her arms back around him and kissed him goodnight. Maybe then she'd know and wouldn't seem so distant.

He sighed. He'd tell her when the time seemed right.

The baseball tournament kept Luke busy throughout the day on Saturday. He met Bridget for lunch, and while they sat together and had burgers, there wasn't any time for a meaningful conversation. Afterward, Luke apologized before returning to the ball field to meet the kids and prepare for their next game. Four other teams from surrounding towns had come out for the tournament.

Luke watched, thinking it odd when Bridget didn't even wander down for a moment or two to watch Angie play. He supposed the booth kept her tied in place and felt guilty for encouraging her to do it and not having the time to assist her as he had planned. He hadn't counted on having Sonya on his heels all day and was grateful for her help with the kids since Bridget was busy with her vendor booth.

In the evening, when it got dark, most booths started packing up. The festival ended with the fireworks there in the park. Luke's team came in second overall in the tournament. Filled with pride, he sought out Bridget for supper. Lisa surprised him by picking up their mother from the nursing home and bringing her for supper at the church.

She'd saved enough seats for all but Bridget. When Luke offered to move to another place, Bridget waved him off and went to sit with the two sisters, Marlene and Maeve. "Sit down, Luke. Enjoy your supper," Lisa smiled, their mother between them.

On the other side of Lisa was Sonya.

"Where's Jimmy?" Little Lizzy wanted to know.

Sonya forked a piece of roast beef. "He got tired, sweetie.

Too long of a day. My brother took him home to stay with my dad for the rest of the evening."

Luke's mother glanced over at Sonya. "You're staying for the fireworks, aren't you?"

"Oh yes," Sonya said, "I'd not miss them. It took all I could to get Jimmy's doctor to agree to let him come home so I wouldn't miss it."

Luke exchanged a look between Lisa and Sonya. He glanced overhead of her to where Bridget sat.

"You'll be joining us, ain't that right, Luke?" Lisa asked.

"Sure." Luke finished with his plate. "I'd best check to see if Bridget needs help loading anything else before it starts."

Lisa gave Sonya a look.

"You're a good boy, Luke. So helpful." His mother patted his arm.

"You need anything, Mom?" Luke checked before he scooted away.

Lisa caught him. "I told Sonya you'd take her home after the fireworks if she stayed."

"Lisa." He tried not to get mad. "You know I've got Bridget and have stuff to unload tonight. You take her home."

Lisa crossed her arms. "I can't. I've got Momma and the girls."

Luke lifted his cap and brushed his hand through his hair. "Fine. But from now on, I'd appreciate you checking with me before you commit me to things."

"Bridget can ride with us girls while you take Sonya home. That way, it ain't awkward for either of them."

"Why would it be awkward?" Luke hissed, keeping his voice low as Mrs. Gavin walked past to put her empty plate in the trash.

"You don't think it's awkward for Sonya having that woman around? You're too good for her, and she knows it. If you keep fooling around, Sonya will move on without you."

"There isn't anything between Sonya and me." Luke

glared at Lisa. "You mind your business, Lisa before you bring trouble."

"The only one in trouble is you, Luke."

"I don't mess in your personal life, and you stay out of mine." He shoved his cap down on his head and headed towards Bridget.

17

All Bridget looked forward to the whole day was spending time with Luke and seeing the fireworks. Although Anne tried to reassure her the thoughts in her head weren't true, Bridget's doubts gnawed at her. She watched as Luke and his family ate supper in the church basement with Sonya and her son.

They all looked so cozy together, a family, and Bridget didn't want to put a wedge in that if that was God's will. She wasn't a home breaker. Even though the little RV was a place to sleep, it wasn't a real home. Not that she could stay there year-round.

While she sat and had supper with Marlene and Maeve, she tried not to focus on Luke with Sonya. She prayed about it the night before but found little peace. Her heart twisted.

She found him on a blanket with Sonya and the girls. Angie held one of her dolls, and Lizzy couldn't sit still waiting for the fireworks. Luke's mom sat in a lawn chair beside Lisa, and Bridget couldn't bring herself to interfere. She had to accept Luke might not feel the same way about her as she did him. She sought Anne and rode home with her after the fireworks.

Unable to sleep, she wandered in the pasture fields. The

old broken equipment and other people's junk cast dark shadows and reminders of the things that can't be fixed.

On a warm, humid night, Romeo and Misty stood under the moon, sleeping. At first, Bridget wondered if they were awake, but Luke told her horses could sleep standing up, and she thought he'd been joking.

Either way, she sat near them, not wanting to spook them, and stared at the stars in the sky. Together she and Luke had traced out several of the constellations and counted way more than they could keep track of.

Living out on a farm wasn't at all like the city. She never ventured out in the dark alone when she lived in Lexington. And here you could see the sky, no tall buildings blocking the view. A bit of moon hung to her left, and Bridget rested her chin on her knees. *Oh Lord*, she prayed, *I don't know what I'm doing here. I don't even know why I feel the way I do. I know better than to get silly over a man. You can't trust them.* And a piece of her heart squeezed. She trusted Luke. She loved him.

Maybe if she had told him?

"Not one for fireworks?" Luke's voice came from her right. She glanced over, her heart going into overdrive.

"Shouldn't you be in bed? Past your bedtime, isn't it?" Luke always had a way of ending their evenings by ten, saying he couldn't stay up past then. But in the dark, she couldn't see if he was smiling at her attempt to tease him.

"I'd say the same thing about you. You know you shouldn't be out here at night alone. I got worried when I couldn't find you during the fireworks. I would have left sooner, but I had to take Sonya home."

The mention of the other woman's name made her flinch. She hadn't meant to. She wanted Luke to be happy. "I'm sure she appreciated having you all to herself."

Luke settled down in front of her. "My mom always says how things work out for the greater good."

Bridget tried to ignore how close he sat to her. In the dark, she couldn't read his expression. "Gram used to say something along the same lines. I can't say how things always end up for the good."

Luke placed his hand on her knee. "I've been waiting for a chance to be alone with you all day. If I hadn't taken Sonya home, I wouldn't have gotten that opportunity now."

"You want to be alone with me, Luke Myers?"

"Been looking forward to it all day." Then his voice dropped, and Bridget would have given anything for a flashlight to see if his ears turned red when he realized what she'd implied. He cleared his throat. "You know what I mean."

Bridget tilted her head. "Do I?"

Luke took off his hat and fiddled with it in his hands. His one knee bent as he spoke. "I've been doing a lot of thinking about us."

"Don't." Bridget decided it was safer to stop him before he broke her heart more. "I'll be out of your way by tomorrow afternoon."

Luke's head jerked up. "Tomorrow? Afternoon?"

"You don't need to worry about me anymore. I'll be out of the RV. I've made enough to pay Shelby most of the rent money I owe her."

She got up, but Luke grabbed her hand. "You'd go back to Lexington?"

Bridget's throat tightened. She shook her head, then stopped. He couldn't see the movement in the dark. "No."

She shook off his hand. "You'll have more time to spend with Sonya and Jimmy without me around to have to worry about. I'd like to keep the bicycle if that's okay with you."

"What are you talking about?" Luke growled on his feet in two seconds. "The bicycle is yours. I gave it to you."

"Thank you." She managed to get the words out. It would have been much easier to slip away in the morning like she had planned.

She walked so fast that she practically ran across the field.

Once in the RV, she secured the door and slid down the back of it in a heap of tears. Why did doing the right thing always have to feel horrible? Bridget buried her face in her hands and cried.

~

When Bridget opened the RV door the following day, the last person she had been expecting was Luke. "Anne won't be making it over this morning. One of the boys isn't feeling well."

"Oh." Biting her lip, she leaned on the door, trying not to show her disappointment. "I hope he is okay."

"Probably all the heat and running around and too much ice cream," Luke said.

Bridget glanced behind him. No Lizzy or Angie this morning. Just her and Luke. She hadn't taken the time to look in the tiny mirror of the RV's bathroom, but her eyes felt like she'd washed them with grit, and her cheeks grew tender. She hoped Luke wasn't the kind of guy to take notice. Maybe he'd think she had a sunburn. He seemed concerned about her getting all red. Only before Sonya returned, Bridget's stomach did a twist while she tried to swallow, feeling grief and nausea at the same time.

She'd known Shelby for years, and while she and Anne had become quick friends ... Luke. She gazed at him feeling about to cry. Luke was her best friend. Not just that, he was the first guy she dreamed of having a future with. A dream, not hers to have. *Oh Lord, why did You have to let me fall in love with this man when he's not mine to have?*

Luke took off his hat. "Bridget, I feel like something has gone amiss these past few days. Have I done something? You know ... To offend you?"

Bridget took a deep breath. This wasn't a conversation she had been wanting to have with him. Not with those soul-searching eyes of his locked on hers. She tried to keep her gaze from falling on those lips. Her brain replayed how they felt pressed to hers, and the butterflies she caged up again inside her went flying. She could hear Anne in her mind telling her to tell him. What did she have to lose? Her grandma always said it was better.

"It's not you, Luke."

"Why don't I believe that? I find you in the field alone. You're leaving. Anne called, saying she couldn't pick you up. Don't we always ride together to church, or were you gonna skip church and take off without saying goodbye?"

She wouldn't point out to him. They rode everywhere together unless Bridget rode her bike. Especially when she saw the look of hurt flash in his hazel eyes, she felt guilty for being responsible for putting it there. Not as much as the hurt slicing her heart.

"I don't think I feel up to going to church today. I need some time to sort a few things out." The thought of riding to church with Luke this morning made her feel worse. The last thing she needed was to sit in the same pew with Sonya on the other side of him, and not having gotten her heart back in a place, she couldn't bear it.

Marlene told her to come anytime. Sooner rather than later suited her heart just fine.

"Is it Lisa? Because if she said something to you, I've already confronted her."

Bridget pushed out a tentative smile. As much as she couldn't figure out why his sister had a thing against her, it wasn't Lisa. "No, it has nothing to do with Lisa."

Luke put his foot on the first stair leading up into the RV. Confusion remained in his features. She could see in the pained expression growing in his eyes he chose his words carefully. "Before Anne called, I thought I'd spend some time with the Lord a different way this morning. Been around many people the past few days and figured some quiet time this morning was due. I'd like it if you'd join me."

Chagrin climbed up her neck and face as he held his hand out to her. She wanted to blurt out her love and hurt feelings for Sonya, but the words stuck in her throat.

Luke was a friend, a good friend. If they could be nothing more, she'd find a way to hold on to his friendship, cherish it even.

"Won't people be expecting you this morning?" she asked.

"Just God and I don't think he'd mind if we spent the morning together, do you?"

Bridget shook her head. She took his hand and walked down the steps to the ground. She wished she could wipe away the last remains of the hurt in his eyes, lingering as he looked at her.

"You think you're ready to ride Romeo on your own this time? I'll saddle him up for you. Unless you want to ride together again?"

Luke appeared determined, and she had a deep suspicion Anne had put him up to clear things up between them.

How she wanted to believe with all her heart they stood a chance! She couldn't have him thinking she was the kind always to run away. That was precisely what she was doing. Grandma wouldn't be proud of her for leaving when things got hard. Bridget sighed. "If I get on Romeo, are you walking with me?"

Luke put on his hat. "Sure am. I'll be on Misty."

Bridget nodded. "And I'll have a saddle this time?"

"Yes, Ma'am."

"And you're sure you want to skip out on service this morning? Won't Sonya be looking for you, and what about your momma?" She hated bringing up the other woman's name.

Luke frowned. "We can visit Momma later."

"Sonya?" She flinched, waiting for his answer.

"Her father and her brother will see after her and Jimmy." He leaned closer for Bridget to get a whiff of his clean scent from a shower.

"I'm sorry we didn't get to sit together and watch the fireworks last night." He searched her face, and Bridget felt her cheeks warm. Part of her wanted him to kiss her, while the other said he wasn't hers to be kissing.

"I didn't want to intrude. You and Sonya seemed cozy, and your momma was happy to be with you all."

Now he did look concerned. "If I made you think there was anything between Sonya and me, it wasn't intentional. Sonya is a friend."

"Just like we're friends?" Bridget shouldn't have said that. She shook her head. "You don't have to explain anything to me, Luke. I told you before I don't need friends."

"Good." Luke took her hands. "Because I don't want to be *just your friend*, Bridget. I'd like to be more if you'll let me."

Bridget's throat closed. She didn't know how she pushed the words out. "Like best friends?"

"Like I want you to know, you can always come to me about anything. I want you to know that I'm always here for you, that you can depend on me." Luke shook his head. "I don't enjoy seeing you upset, and I'm sorry if what I'm about to say causes you distress. But I love you." His hand went up to her face and smoothed his thumb over her tender, warm cheek.

His words broke the thin shield she constructed overnight. Her eyes brimmed with tears, and her mouth spilled out the words she had wanted to tell him. "I love you, too."

18

The sun had changed to a bronze globe of orange in the evening sky when Luke escorted Bridget over to Pete and Anne's house for another Sunday evening get-together.

"There's Anne. I'm going to go over and check on the boys and see if I can help." Bridget slid her hand from his. He hugged her back, leaned down, and kissed her. She gave him a playful shove and walked off toward Anne in the kitchen.

"Hey, Luke! Over here!" Pete waved.

Luke's gaze followed the familiar voice until he spotted Pete by the grill. In the yard, the kids played tag, and neighbors stood in small groups and chatted. He spotted Sonya with her brother, and Lisa gave him the stink eye. He glared right back before turning to Pete.

"Missed you this morning," Pete said, holding his hand for Luke to shake.

"Bridget and I rode through the fields and down the old gas well roads. We needed to talk."

"I am sure you did." Sam came up, a bottle of water in one hand. "Thought you'd have dumped her at the bus station by now."

Luke couldn't help narrowing his gaze on Sam.

"What Sam's trying to say is that we know Bridget might leave town soon," Pete said.

"Leaving town?" She would have told him. Or was that what she intended packing her things for Anne to pick her up? Luke glanced through the sliding glass window at Anne and Bridget. She caught his glance and smiled at him.

"I don't think so." Luke looked at Pete and then at Sam. "What has my sister been saying now?"

Pete and Sam exchanged looks as Sonya strolled up behind him. Her eyes filled with sympathy. "I'm sorry, Luke, for what the woman did to you." She went to wrap her arms around him, and he stepped away.

"What are you talking about?" Then he glowered over at Lisa. She appeared crestfallen and shook her head. "Listen, I don't know what Lisa's saying now, but...."

"You're a better man than I could be." Sam interrupted. "You forgave her, didn't you?"

Luke reined in his imagination. "Of course, I forgive her. She's my sister." Luke replied with a tight smile. He wasn't about to discuss his opinions of his sister with anyone, even though Pete and Sam were good friends.

"Listen, Luke, what if I told you that there's — um — somewhere else she's planning to go, and she kind of used your funds to set herself up?"

"I'd say you've been hanging around my sister too much, and you need to ignore the rumors and mind your own business." Luke had heard everything Lisa was saying to people and knew she wanted Bridget gone. Her feelings threatened by having an outsider want to stay here was something he'd taken up with God on many a night. His sister would have to work through it.

"What if I could prove it? Or at least Lisa can?" Sonya prompted.

"Prove what?" Luke crossed his arms as Sonya walked from around him to face him.

"Well, you can verify it with Brenda at the bank, but Bridget got a check written out and sent it to Lexington to pay rent. Ms. Harding watched her put the stamp on it."

Pete wore a dire expression. "She asked Anne to get her stuff this morning. Anne didn't feel right about helping her leave."

"I can see how this looks," Luke said. "I appreciate your concern for me, but it was a misunderstanding."

"So, she didn't take your money, and she's not going back to Lexington?" Sam asked.

"No and no." Luke sighed. "Look, Bridget owed past rent from where she'd been living in Lexington. She's been sending money to pay the debt. As far as moving out of the RV … she's staying now. It was a misunderstanding. We cleared it up this morning."

"Good." Pete's expression lightened, but he didn't think Sam was convinced, and Sonya seemed displeased by it.

"What exactly did you clear up?" Lisa joined them.

Anne and Bridget stepped out from the sliding glass doors. Anne handed Pete a chicken platter as Bridget set another plate of burgers by the grill. Luke slid his arm around her and pulled her close. "That Bridget and I are dating."

"Does that mean she's your girlfriend?" Leave it to Lizzy to scoot out around him. A big crooked, toothy grin on her face.

Bridget glanced at Luke. Her smile tightened as she tensed. He knew she was nervous standing there with his proclamation hanging in the air. Luke brushed his hand over Lizzy's hair. "Sure does."

Lisa's eyes widened. "How can you do that with Sonya standing right here?"

"Don't think I don't know or appreciate what you've been trying to do," Sonya said to Lisa with a shrug. "We were always better friends."

And Luke nodded. "Friends."

Sonya glanced away. "I should go check on Jimmy."

Bridget laid her hand on Luke's arm. "I'm sorry," she said to Sonya.

"Nothing to be sorry about. I just hope we can start over and be friends, too," Sonya said.

"I'd like that." Bridget leaned her head against Luke's arm.

Anne leaned against Pete as he finished arranging burgers on the grill. She gave him a little hip bump. "Told you."

"How convenient. Next, you'll be telling us you're going to marry her," Lisa huffed.

"Eventually." Luke kept a tight hold on Bridget. He hadn't mentioned the 'M' word to her. They'd only said 'I love you' that morning, and he didn't want to rush her and scare her into leaving him.

Thank the Lord she hadn't laughed at him. His heart still beat wildly, remembering her sweet words in return.

"Well. If that's the way of it, she'd better find somewhere else to stay. What will people think, her staying on the farm and you on the farm and not married." Lisa tilted her chin up.

Anne laughed. "Oh, Lisa, you sound just like my great-grandmother. But I assure you, had Junior not been feeling bad this morning, I would have helped Bridget take care of that minor detail."

Luke sucked in a breath. Bridget squeezed his arm. "I meant to tell you. I figured I'd wait until later. I'm still moving out of the RV. Lisa's right, Luke. I can't keep living there. But I'm not going far. Marge's got the bed-and-breakfast in town. She could use some help keeping up with it, and she's got a floral shop in the front. I'm going to stay there, but I'll be over every day to help run our business and … and see you."

"So, you're just moving in with Marge here in town?"

Bridget nodded.

"And you knew this?" He glanced at Pete and Anne.

Guilty expressions appeared on their faces as they nodded.

"And this morning?"

Anne spoke up. "Jayden didn't feel well, but it wasn't as bad as I made it out to be. I'm sorry."

"I already forgave Anne," Bridget said, "And now I don't think there is any more misunderstanding between us." She wrapped both her arms around Luke. "You understand why I'm going to stay with Marlene, right?"

Luke kissed her cheek. "Yeah, I do. I don't like it, but I do."

"Then you'll have to convince her to marry you sooner rather than later," Sam chuckled.

"I can do that." Luke gazed into her eyes. "How's a week from Tuesday?"

Bridget leaned back. "Hold your horses there, cowboy." Her voice squeaked.

"Okay, the last Friday of next month."

"To get married?" Bridget's brows rose into her hairline.

"No, for me to propose."

She sighed and relaxed into his arms. "How about we take this new friendship one day at a time?"

"I can do that, too," Luke said.

"Lizzy! Angie! Come on. We're leaving." Lisa glared at them both and stepped off the deck. Luke heard the girls whining, and Bridget went to move away from him when he stopped her. "Let her go."

Anne agreed. "She'll adjust. Give her time."

Luke watched Lisa take the girls and leave. He prayed for God to help her deal with her hurts and insecurities about relationships and past hurts to accept and make room in her heart for him and Bridget's future.

19

For weeks, Bridget helped Marge around the bed-and-breakfast and Anne occasionally in the mornings. Luke would come to pick her up by lunchtime and take her to the farm.

He got her a driver's booklet, and she took the written part of the test to get her driver's license. Luke insisted on teaching her to drive. Eventually, it would get too cold, Luke told her to ride a bike between the farm and town.

Some evenings, he took her out on the back roads and let her drive his truck. And then other evenings, they rode horseback or sat and talked during the sun setting over the horizon.

She missed the girls at the farm, Lisa only left them with Luke a few days a week, and school would start for Angie at the end of the month.

On Sundays, they visited Luke's mother after church and walked in the park. He'd gotten a new laptop for her to take between Marlene's and the barn for handling her online shop for their business. Thanks to all the sales coming in, she sent the last payment to Shelby for the rent, not even a thank you in response.

Oddly, Bridget found she was okay with it. Hidden Hills

was the last place she ever thought to end up, but the thought of going away, leaving Luke, struck a sharp pain in her heart. She loved him too much.

"Ready?" Luke came around the barn with Lizzy from feeding the goats.

"Another driving lesson?" She winced, thinking how she scraped the door of Luke's truck on a fence post the last time she tried driving and got too close between the pasture gates.

"I thought we'd drive into Shelbyville tonight, do something special."

Lizzy stood beside him and beamed. "Can I go?"

"Not this time, Pumpkin," Luke said, looking at Bridget, pinning her with his blue-eyed gaze.

Bridget brushed her hands down over her jean-clad hips. "I guess I should get cleaned up. Will Lisa be home soon for the girls?"

"We've got an hour."

Those words sent a ripple of joy, coursing through her. She glanced over at Angie and then at Lizzy again. Holding out her hand, she said to Lizzy, "We'd best help Angie and get our mess cleaned up before it's time to go."

"Go. Do what you need to do. I'll be waiting."

It stirred in her belly, the anticipation of his words. Bridget ducked her head and took Lizzy's hand, going in the barn.

Lizzy plopped down on a pile of clothes and fabric Bridget and Luke had brought home from one of his trips to another town. They found it in a dumpster behind an old textile company that told them they could have it.

She praised Angie for her work as they sorted by color and cloth type and folded it. Lizzy gave up after a bit, laying down atop the pile and making them pull out from under her.

Angie giggled until Lizzy curled up in a ball near Bridget and napped. At first, Bridget thought the little girl pretended until gentle snores reached her ears. Angie pressed a hand over her mouth and giggled.

On a hot summer like this, Bridget wanted to lie down too and rest, but the knots in her belly and the thought of going to Shelbyville with Luke wouldn't let her.

"Momma won't like her sleeping before bed," Angie said.

"A quick nap won't hurt. We'll wake her before you have to go to the house." Bridget picked up a long piece of upholstery fabric. She inventoried in her mind thinking it would look nice over that high-back chair Luke brought home the day she met him.

"My momma doesn't hate you," Angie said, catching Bridget off guard.

Bridget lost her grin. "What makes you say that?"

"My grandma says that sometimes when we're afraid of something, it makes us mad."

"Why would your momma be afraid of me?" Bridget put down the piece of fabric she was folding.

Angie shrugged. "I think it has to do with going away to be with my daddy. He went away and left her alone, and nobody was nice to her, so she came here with us."

Bridget put her arm around the little girl, and held her close. All the while, her heart tore for Lisa. "I'm sorry that happened."

"You are not leaving Uncle Luke, are you?" Angie glanced up at her, her eyes filled with sincerity.

"I couldn't if I wanted to," Bridget confessed.

"Why is that?"

Bridget pressed her finger to the little girl's lip. "Can you keep a secret?"

Angie nodded.

She leaned in and whispered in Angie's ear. "I think your Uncle Luke will ask me to marry him."

Bridget tilted away to see Angie's lips formed a smile. "Are you gonna say yes?"

Bridget nodded. In her heart, she knew she was ready to be Luke's wife.

Angie's smile went upside down. "You could still leave. My daddy did."

"Oh, sweetie. I know, but he'll be back. Your momma's a very strong woman. Her heart must have been breaking all this time, having him gone, and we're going to have to keep praying for God to heal it."

She took her finger away, and Angie said, "I pray all the time for Daddy to come home."

"Well, maybe he will if we invite him to the wedding?"

Angie's eyes brightened. "Really? Do you think?"

"He might not if he's stationed overseas, but we can invite him. And you can help me make the invites."

"Yes! Please? Can I?" Angie bounced.

"Shh …" Bridget glanced over at Lizzy, sleeping on the pile of clothes and fabrics they were trying to sort. "Of course."

"What is all this?" Luke came in.

Angie shushed him. "You gonna wake Lizzy, and we've got wedding invites to make. Bridget said we can invite Daddy."

"Whoa there. Invites to a wedding?" Luke scowled. "How do you even know I'm going to ask?"

Angie grinned. "Oh, come on, Uncle Luke. We know you looove her!"

Then Luke chuckled. "Yeah, I suppose. But a man likes to ask the girl before she plans the wedding."

Bridget got up off the barn floor. Tilting her head, she said, "I assumed you wouldn't mind."

"Not at all." Luke shook his head, "Doug's family. Does this mean you have a date in mind?"

Bridget grinned, sauntering up to him and putting her arms around his waist. "Next spring?"

Luke narrowed his eyes and frowned. Bridget giggled. "I think a fall wedding in late October would be lovely. Nothing fancy."

"Then I'd best get to asking." Luke brushed a strand of hair away from her face. He touched her lips and murmured, "Marry me, Bridget Wilson?"

"I thought you'd never ask," she whispered against his lips.

WHAT'S NEXT?

A nurse and an ex-convict must put their differences aside to stop a drug ring in their town.

When Mariah's mother goes missing and Tanner Evans shows up on her doorstep after all these years, how can she trust it isn't him causing trouble for her family again?

Not able to save one brother, Mariah became a nurse to help save others. Who knew her younger brother would get caught up in drugs or that she'd find herself trapped between doing what is right or holding her family together? **Would Tanner's interference bring more grief to her already broken heart or can these two reckless hearts find a way to reconcile?**

Find out in RECKLESS HEARTS
Keep reading for preview…

SNEAK PEEK OF RECKLESS HEARTS

CHAPTER 1

"Mariah, you got a call on line two, and Doc Harrison needs that suture done at bed twelve."

Mariah finished securing the sling on little Reggie Blake's arm. Poor kid had a black eye and a set of cracked ribs.

Mom stood on the other side of the bed brushing back Reggie's cowlick. He tilted his head trying to avoid her touch.

Mariah went about her business. She felt for the kid, and she understood how young boys had a brain to do stupid things. "All right, you all. Hang tight, and we'll get those discharge papers, Mom."

Mom nodded, a few stray tears trickling down her pale face. Mariah had no doubt eight-year-old Reggie had taken at least a dozen years off his momma's life. She pointed at him. "And don't you come back now. You hear?"

Those eyes, glazed with the onset of pain killers and exhaustion looked so solemnly at her; it nearly broke her heart.

A rustle of the curtain and a shout from Gail, she said to Reggie. "No superman off the roof anymore, promise?"

"Okay." Reggie glanced at his mom.

Mom nodded in agreement. Mariah squeezed Mom's arm as she headed out. "Suture in twelve!"

"I've got it. You get that phone. Sheriff Brady ain't going to stay on that line forever, girl."

Mariah's chest squeezed close. Lengthening her stride, she made her way to the nurses' station. Bending over the counter, she grabbed the phone. "Sheriff."

"Mariah. It's your momma."

"I'm on my way." She slammed down the phone, turned, and found Dr. Harrison in her way. His stout frame made it easy for him to block her. "Running off again, Mariah?"

Dr. Harrison reached behind her, and she didn't have to look to know that Kim had turned to hand him a can of Coca-Cola.

Trying hard not to react to the sound of the tab cracking open as he took a swig and arched his brow at her, Mariah said, "I'm sorry. It's Momma. I've got to go."

"And I've got a patient in bed twelve waiting to have the cut between his toes sewed shut."

"I've got it," Gail walked past, holding up the suture kit.

"Thanks, Gail." Mariah side-stepped out of the way, grateful the words she had been thinking hadn't escaped her mouth. She needed this job. Needed it enough to put up with Dr. Harrison and his Coke-drinking, potato chip-grease fingered bedside manner. She'd once heard him tell a patient not to eat the very thing he stood in front of the man chomping down on. It had taken everything she had not to let him hear her laugh. And she had, at the nurses' station with the other nurses away from his ears.

She'd shake her head later. No wonder the man's wife left him.

No time. Mariah had to get to Momma. What could it be now?

"You'll make it up to me later," Gail called back.

Dr. Harrison narrowed his eyes at her as Mariah slipped

out from between him and the nurses' station. "You'll need someone to cover your shift."

Mariah glanced at her watch, relieved by the time, "Janet will be coming in less than an hour."

Dr. Harrison made a noise in his throat. At the sound of his name, he turned on his heel and headed down the hall.

Taking this opportunity to slip away, Mariah practically ran from the emergency room. Her heart pounded, thinking of what could have happened this time. She grabbed her purse and jacket and was on her way.

The last thing Mariah had said to her brother was to stay home, watch Momma, and she'd call later to check on them.

Did he listen?

Of course not.

Myles had the patience of a rabbit and the mind of a mule. One day it would get him in trouble, but that day wasn't today.

Mariah prayed, hoping her brother had enough sense not to have run off when he knew someone had to stay with Momma. It was bad enough she had to take all the evening and night shifts to give Myles daytime hours to attend school.

She never bothered locking Momma's old sedan in fear the lock would catch as it had a habit of doing and not open when she tried. She could make the drive home blind if needed. With one headlight brighter than the other, she pulled out of the hospital parking lot and made the twenty-five-minute drive home.

As she turned and headed down the old dirt road leading to their farm, a sickening feeling stirred deep in her belly. It had been almost ten years since the accident that took her older brother Mark's life, but every time she drove over the spot, it was like walking across his grave.

As she got closer to the farm lane, she turned off her headlights. Lights glowed up the road in the trees.

What was Tyler Evans up to?

No one had been up to that old hunting cabin in years.

Trying to ignore the tightening of her gut, Mariah drove past the barn and parked out by the old machine shed. A police SUV sat near the house. She no more than got out of her car when the front door opened, and Momma stepped out on the porch, followed by Sheriff Brady.

Momma stood in her pearl snap housecoat and an old pair of Daddy's socks. "I called the police. I told them they were trespassing!"

"I'm sorry, Sheriff." It was all Mariah could think to say to him.

Sheriff Brady pulled back his shoulders and rested his hands on his hips. "There's no one here, Mariah."

"I know." Mariah reached out to take Momma by the arm. "Come on, Momma."

"They're up there again. They're messing behind our barn." Momma pointed out behind the house.

"The barn's on the other side of the lane, Momma. Where's Myles?" Mariah asked.

Sheriff Brady let his shoulder sag as she stepped out of her way to take Momma back in the house.

"Didn't you see the lights? They're up there; up to no good. Something bad is going to happen. I'm telling you they got no business up there. Your father built that cabin."

And Momma went on and on as Mariah got her in her recliner. She put the blanket over Momma's legs. Mariah clicked on the television, and Momma went quiet, switching her attention to the late-night game show.

Mariah put the remote in her mother's hand and squeezed it. "You watch your show, Momma. Don't you worry about it. Ain't nobody up there or around the barn. It's okay."

Then Momma gazed over at Mariah, bending over the chair. "You stay away from that Evans boy, hear? It's bad enough your brother went running off again with that boy. Nothing but trouble."

"I know, Momma." Mariah's heart squeezed. Behind her, Sheriff Brady cleared his throat. She straightened, took a deep breath, and went into the kitchen, leaving Momma to her late-night show. Mariah hoped the show would distract Momma enough to help her fall asleep. Where was Myles?

She was going to kick that younger brother of hers to the next county if he didn't start getting his head on straight. She dropped down into a chair at the table. Her purse slid down from her shoulder to the floor.

At least she'd almost made it to the end of her shift before the call came.

"This is the third time this month, Mariah." Sheriff Brady stood, arms crossed, and used the same stern voice with her as he had when she was in high school. His brows drew together. "Now, you're gonna have to do something about your momma."

"I'm sorry Momma called and disturbed you, Sheriff."

Sheriff Brady's eyes softened. "It's not the calls that bother me, Mariah. I can't keep driving out here for false calls."

"I know. She's lonely is all, and sometimes she forgets." Mariah hung her head. "Myles is supposed to be here. I don't know where he is." Anger burned down her throat and in her gut. At that moment, she could hear a truck coming down the lane. Leave it to Myles to pick a time like this to show up.

"I'll go drive around, probably just Tyler and some buddies drinking around the bonfire up at the cabin on a Friday night."

Mariah swallowed hard and nodded. It felt like a lifetime ago when her older brothers, Matt and Mark, used to invite their friends up there to hang out. How long had it been since she ventured on that side of their property?

"Sheriff, don't you be afraid to cuff those boys of mine when you see them. They know better."

"Oh, I will," Sheriff Brady called out to her, raising a

brow at Mariah. He tilted his head toward the door, and she followed.

A truck pulled in the driveway; in the dark, it was hard to make it out, but it had dual wheels and her brother Myles drove the old Ford F-150.

As the truck parked and the cab lit up with the door opening, Mariah froze on the porch. She blinked to let her vision adjust in the dark, her stomach curling as the light-haired man stepped away from the truck.

"Is that who I think it is?" it came as barely a whisper.

Sheriff Brady adjusted his hat and looked out across the yard to where the pole lamp sent an eerie glow across the grass.

"After your mother called us at the station, she decided to venture up to the cabin on her own. Tanner Evans found her walking down the road near his granddaddy's lane."

Mariah's throat tightened.

Tanner?

Her chest tightened.

Tanner Evans?

It couldn't be.

"You mean Tyler."

"No. Tanner, the younger of the two," Sheriff Brady said.

But that would mean?

Her lungs held all their air, and she managed to squeak out. "What's Tanner doing here?"

The world would spin shortly.

Tanner Evans?

She felt the sting deep in her chest, tried to force out air to breathe again.

"He said he had an errand to run and would stop on his way back to check on Penny."

That couldn't be right. Momma got things mixed up all the time, but the Sheriff?

Oh no. Not Tanner.

Please, Lord, he wasn't ever supposed to come back.

A wad of grief and a decade-old ache erupted from around her heart. She tilted forward a little, tried to keep her lungs from shutting off.

"You gonna be alright?" Tanner stuffed his hands in his pockets and walked up the front steps.

Now that was the billion-dollar question of the night.

Mariah tried not to let the sheriff see the wave of nausea swelling inside her. Her heart beat faster as if to nudge her lungs to get working back to normal again.

Nothing was ever normal around here anymore. And it wouldn't ever be with Tanner Evans back.

If it was Tanner.

She gritted her teeth, looking at the devil himself. At first, she could have mistaken him for Tyler, the two brothers had similar features, but as he came closer under the porch light, there was no mistaking him.

Tanner Evans had returned.

"I take it you can handle things from here." Sheriff Brady squeezed her shoulder and went down the stairs. He gave Tanner a long look after which both men seemed to come to a silent understanding.

She wanted to scream, to shout, for Sheriff to stay. Why was he leaving her when he knew what Tanner had done? Why wasn't he arresting him and taking him far away from here?

"I wasn't sure if you'd be home yet," Tanner said, smooth and calm as ever while every fiber in Mariah's being held taut as she found words to respond. "As you can see, I'm here."

And a dozen different emotions she'd been holding inside her started to crack open. She had nothing to say to him.

For years, she'd tried to put the memories behind her. Forget Tanner. Forgive what he'd done to her—not her, but her brother Mark.

"Your mom okay?"

"She's fine. She gets confused sometimes." Mariah said, grateful when Tanner did not attempt to come up the stairs. He stuffed his hands in his pockets and rocked back on his boot heels. Maybe Momma had been right calling the sheriff. A man like Tanner out this late at night, running errands, had to be up to no good.

By the look of the dark shadow on his chin and his hair cropped a bit shorter than she remembered, there wasn't much else that had changed about him.

"I figured. She wandered over near the creek by our place, and I've found her a few times up by the cabin. I've brought her back more than once. Usually, Myles is here."

It struck her like a paper cut, the pain sharp and quick, causing her to suck in her breath.

Tanner Evans had found Momma?
Had she been going to his farm?
Had he been here before?

"Yeah, he is. Usually."

Hearing the game show on the television inside the house and her chest getting tighter, she bit her lip against the sickening feeling that had started in her stomach.

Tanner was the reason her brother Mark was dead. How on earth was she supposed to be okay?

She glanced at her watch. It was almost eleven o'clock.

"I'd best be getting home. Milking comes early. I'll see you around."

She hugged herself, watching him walk away.

She waited until the truck pulled out of the yard and the lights headed toward the Evans' Dairy Farm to sit on the step and bury her face in her hands.

When the cold set in her bones, Mariah went back in the house; Momma didn't sleep much at night anymore. She couldn't blame Myles for falling asleep if he'd been here at all. She sat and watched *The Price is Right* until she heard the truck pull in the yard well past midnight.

Mariah gritted her teeth, glancing back at Momma and then got up to greet the tall, lanky man who stepped inside the kitchen door.

If looks could kill, she would have had Myles pinned against the wall in a flash.

The silence stretched as Mariah fought to push her anger down. She'd let it brew since Tanner left.

Myles took one look at her and muttered a curse.

"Watch your mouth; Momma's awake."

Myles peeked in the living room. "She's always awake this time of night."

"Which is why you're supposed to be here with her." Mariah glared harder at him. "Where have you been?"

"Mark, is that you?" Momma called from the living room.

Myles moved past her to the doorway and said, "No, Momma, it's Myles."

Then Momma went back to her show. Mariah stood with her hand on her hip, and her anger churned from a low-grade burn to full fury.

Myles turned with his hands up. "Don't even go there, Mariah."

"Where were you? It's past midnight! I had to leave my shift early. Do you know what that means?"

"So, you left early." Myles shrugged. "Unlike you, some of us have a life." Myles walked into the living room.

"We have a deal. You go to school during the day and stay with Momma at night while I work."

"No, Mariah. You're the one who said I would stay with Momma at night. I have a life, and it ain't stuck on this farm."

"You sound just like Matt." Mariah glanced over at Momma, her eyes drifting off to sleep as if her children weren't standing in the same room with her yelling at each other.

"Why do you think I work nights so you can go to school during the day? Do you think I like working the night shift?

Or twelve hour days sometimes? I do it for you and Momma."

"Well, nobody asked you to." Myles headed for the stairs.

"Myles?" Momma was wide awake.

"Yeah, Ma?" He said, not bothering looking back.

"It's past your bedtime. You need something?" Momma asked.

"I'm good, Momma." Myles headed up the stairs.

Mariah sighed. A hand reached out and touched her arm. "You out with that boy again tonight? It's about time you got home."

There was no sense in arguing. "I'm home, Momma. Don't you worry. I ain't going anywhere."

SNEAK PEEK OF RECKLESS HEARTS
CHAPTER 2

Every morning was the same old story. Tanner stretched with a cup of steaming coffee in hand, sending a curl of white mist from the lip of his travel mug as he made his way from the house to the barn. Old Matilda bawled, and the other cows moved restlessly inside the barn. A peek of the sun bled over the pastures, through the trees with golden hues and red highlights of autumn making its mark.

He yawned, Tanner could have done for at least another hour of sleep, having been up most of the night checking on one of the heifers about to freshen. Poor thing had been showing signs of labor for two days.

He had started chasing her in from the pasture late last night when he found Mrs. Lehman out on one of her wanderings. She'd gone with him when he found her out in the dark.

She chatted away, in her motherly fashion, as if nothing had ever happened between her family and his all those years ago.

His gut twisted, and not from Pap's black wake up juice.

His brother, Tyler, leaned against the milk house with his hand stretched out. "Pap said there would be frost in the morning."

Tanner gave him the vicious brew their grandfather concocted every morning and called it coffee. "Things are bound to warm up around here sooner or later."

"Is that so?" Tyler took a sip of his coffee and winced. "You know when you got back, you said you were sticking to the farm, but then you were out pretty late last night. What's her name?"

"Dora."

"Where she from?"

"She's one of ours. I had to chase her in from the pasture last night before she dropped her calf out in the field. You can find her and little September in the far back pen in the barn."

"Wait." Tyler held up his hand. "You named the calf September? Serious man?"

"Born in September, named it September."

Tyler shook his head. "You need a life. You're getting as bad as Pap naming those animals."

He had a life, a long time ago, when he'd been young and stupid. He thought long and hard about coming back to Hidden Hills, and couldn't think of anywhere else he'd go. He'd tried to prepare himself for all the changes, but not much had changed. Especially Mariah. After all these years, she looked as pretty as she did back in high school.

Rather than dwell on what was and what couldn't happen, he changed the subject. "Where did you go last night? I could have used your help chasing in that heifer."

"Out at Luke Myers' place, welding new blades on Ben's old plow. He busted two, and Luke had an older model up in his equipment graveyard. I stayed until about ten then came home to crash. Four a.m. comes early," Tyler held up his coffee.

"So, you weren't up at the old cabin?"

"On the Lehman place? I wouldn't be caught dead there." Tyler flinched, he reached up and pulled down his knit cap over his head. "I didn't mean—"

Tanner waved if off. "No big. Mrs. Lehman claimed she heard someone up there. She was out last night, and I found her when I went to retrieve Dora."

"Ain't that like the second time you've been over there?" Tyler narrowed his gaze.

"Third."

"You think that's a good idea?"

"What did you want me to do? Leave her out wandering the woods at night?"

"I can't say I wouldn't have done the same thing. You see Mariah?"

"Yeah."

Tyler sat his cup of joe on his truck hood. "You're alive, so?"

"So, Mrs. Lehman called the sheriff."

"How did that go?" Tyler asked.

"I left as soon as the sheriff showed up. I figured it was best, and I had to see to Dora since you weren't around. I stopped back to check on her and figured Myles would be there, but it was Mariah."

"Bet she was happy to see you."

From inside the milk house, Pap shouted. "Cows ain't gonna milk themselves."

"I guess that's our call to get a moooove on," Tyler chuckled at his lame joke and tipped up the coffee to his lips. Tanner shook his head and moved past him.

Mariah had seemed anything but happy to see him. Not that he could blame her, bad blood between them and all. He tried to get her out of his head. Spent years trying not to think of her or that moment when he'd see her again. Not that it mattered much. There wouldn't ever be anything between them.

The night he wrecked Mark's Pontiac Grand AM had sealed their fate.

He breathed in the crisp air of grain and manure. He

listened to the hum of the compressor warming up, and it grounded him back to reality.

"The fence out in the back forty near the Lehman's place is down again. After we get cleaned up here, I'll need you to give me a hand. Maybe you could ride up to the cabin and take a look around. I doubt the sheriff went up there, seeing as Mrs. Lehman gets confused sometimes."

"I wouldn't think you'd want to go back there. It's probably a bunch of teenagers having a kegger."

"Which is why someone needs to make sure no one ever gets hurt up there again."

Tyler's response was drowned by the sound of the compressor kicking on in the milk house. Its loud buzz calling the herd as they shuffled and shoved in the waiting pen. If they didn't get the first batch of cows in the stanchions soon, Pap would curse them up a storm for all the milk going to waste. Tanner rolled the sleeves of his flannel shirt to his elbows and went to bring the cows in.

Down in the pit of the milking parlor, a wrinkled and white bushy-haired man stood scowling at them both. "Can't keep the ladies waiting for you boys; let's get a move on. We've got a day of chores ahead of us."

"Maybe he does," Tyler bumped Tanner in the arm.

Tyler whistled as he took the steps to the pit. He sat the travel mug on the top of the cement stairs and grabbed the washrag, rolling back his shoulders, "Let'm in."

It took a little over two hours to milk them all, switching six cows on each side. Tanner did the washing, Pap swinging the milkers, and Tyler filling the feeders and swapping the cows through the chutes. At the end of leading the last bunch of cows back out, Tyler had slipped outside to feed a few calves and disappeared.

He could hear the rumble of the diesel engine as Tyler left for work. Farming had never been in his older brother's blood. Tyler's talents were in his trade of welding.

Inside the milk house, the sounds of the compressor shut off, and Pap stepped out, wiping his aged hands in a rag before tucking it in the back pocket of his pants. He grunted and pointed a gnarled finger. "Long night. You catch some z's before you try working on that fence. We don't need no accidents around here."

"No, Pap. No accidents."

"Tyler." His grandfather shouted.

"He's gone already."

Pap's face scrunched up. "Don't you forget to clean out the back pens." Then Pap shuffled his way past Tanner toward the old farmhouse. "Bacon will be ready in a bit."

And he knew better than to argue.

The scent of Pap's burnt bacon and fresh farm eggs in the morning had been a welcome aroma compared to the powdered eggs and processed stuff served in prison.

He might have served his time, but people wouldn't ever forget.

Either way, he'd lost his best friend that day.

He didn't think Mark's sister would ever forgive him.

He'd seen most of the Lehmans since coming home six months ago. It was kind of hard to avoid them being in a small town like Hidden Hills.

Not feeling hungry, he headed around toward the machine shed.

"Breakfast is in the other direction," Tyler said, stepping out of the milk house.

"I heard the truck. I thought you left."

"I parked it behind the barn. I need to unload those new gates for out in the back forty. I am off today, so I thought we could get that done before Pap started harping on us."

"I'm taking the four-wheeler out to check the fence in the heifer field. I'll meet you there in a couple of hours. We might as well work our way forward."

"You sure about this?" Tyler asked.

"Somebody's got to fix it. Those new gates will be the least of our worries if a cow gets loose and wanders over to the Lehman's."

"True. But we don't want Pap having a heart attack either." Tyler punched Tanner in the shoulder. "Take your cell phone with you."

Tanner patted his front pocket. "Always."

Inside the machine shed, Tanner checked the gas and pulled the four-wheeler. He took the fence line and followed it around the pasture that connected his grandfather's land to the Lehman's.

Not far out, he spotted a maroon SUV going down through the woods. He sat and idled, watching it leave the direction of the cabin. Taking out his phone, he snapped a quick picture.

Driving farther up the pasture and away from the vehicle, Tanner parked it near the broken fence and went to inspect the section. They had recently replaced the posts; he and Tyler had put them in not long after his release, and they'd strung up new wire.

Tanner picked up the end of a broken strand.

It wasn't electric, but the high-tension wire strung between the posts had been cut, and Tanner slipped his phone back in his pocket. He walked through the opening in the fence and into the woods. He spotted the roofline of the cabin. Smoke curled from the chimney.

ABOUT THE AUTHOR

Growing up on a farm in Pennsylvania, Susan Lower yearned for adventure. A woodsy gal, Susan prefers camping over going to the beach any day. Still a farm girl at heart, Susan writes fast action reads filled with cowboys, heroes, and hope. She writes both western historical and contemporary romances, romantic suspense, and has been itching to one day write a mystery or thriller. Christmas is her favorite holiday, and she loves to write resilient characters struggling to overcome the complications of life while holding their values and strengthening their faith.

www.ingramcontent.com/pod-product-compliance
Lightning Source LLC
Chambersburg PA
CBHW022124170626
46808CB00002B/827